Als
Chantal Fernando

Angels & Devil MC Series

Love Grudge

The Knights & Dragons MC Series

Decker's Dilemma
Rhett Redeemed

The Fast & Fury Series

Custom Built
Custom Made
Custom Love

The Knights of Fury MC Series

Saint
Renegade
Temper

The Wind Dragons MC Series

Dragon's Lair
Arrow's Hell
Tracker's End
Dirty Ride
Rake's Redemption
Wild Ride
Wolf's Mate
Last Ride
Crossroads

The Cursed Ravens MC Series

Ace of Hearts
Knuckle Down
Going Rogue

The Conflict of Interest Series

Breaching the Contract
Seducing the Defendant
Approaching the Bench
Leading the Witness

LOVE BETRAYAL

CHANTAL FERNANDO

carina
press

Recycling programs
for this product may
not exist in your area.

ISBN-13: 978-1-335-45458-4

Love Betrayal

Carina Press
22 Adelaide St. West, 41st Floor
Toronto, Ontario M5H 4E3, Canada
www.CarinaPress.com

Printed in U.S.A.

For Tahj,

My up-and-coming fighter,
musical genius and my protector.

Love you always

LOVE
BETRAYAL

Prologue

River

One Year Ago

As I step inside the bar, I tap the back pocket of my dark jeans to make sure I remembered to bring my wallet in from the car. My cousin Romeo and I will no doubt fight to pay the tab, like we always do, as if who pays is the biggest alpha in the room.

As I follow Romeo in, I see who he stops to talk to.

"I'm…fuck." I stop abruptly.

Julianna Callisto.

The daughter of the president of the Angels Motorcycle Club, someone who is supposed to be Romeo's sworn enemy.

"Nice to meet you, Fuck," Julianna replies with attitude, and Romeo laughs. It's a familiar laugh, and I feel like I've missed a fucking chapter in what is going on right now. He's into her.

"This is River," he says, nodding to me.

Julianna is beautiful. Blonde hair. Full lips. And a body men would fall over themselves for. Clearly Romeo has already fallen.

Yet my eyes are instantly drawn to the woman next to her. The one I don't know. I keep my sight on her, like a lion with its prey. "And who are you?"

"I'm Bella," she says, her sweet voice making my cock twitch. With her long dark hair and almond-shaped gray eyes, she is one of the most strikingly beautiful women I've ever seen.

"You're not a Callisto, are you?" I ask, hoping that getting her into my bed isn't going to come with a fuck load of trouble.

"Sorry to disappoint," she replies, with a sexy smirk.

"Ah, fuck," I mutter, but still find myself sitting down next to her. Next to us, Romeo is getting awfully close to Julianna, so I guess this is how tonight is playing out. We may be cousins, but he's also my best friend and I always have his back. Even when he's making questionable choices. "Guess we are all making bad decisions tonight. Can I buy you a drink?"

She smiles.

When she looks away, I lean closer and breathe in the scent of her hair. Vanilla with a hint of cinnamon.

And in that moment, I know that it's all over for me.

It's not long before Romeo and Julianna leave the

bar, and I'm wondering what the fuck he is thinking, but also distracted by the woman next to me. Bella had pulled Julianna aside before they left, probably asking her what the fuck she is doing, like a good friend, but they left together anyway. Romeo makes me promise to get Bella home safely, and of course I would have done that anyway. I might be capable of many things, some of them would be illegal in the eyes of the law, but hurting a woman isn't one of them. Besides, her hair smells so good and I want to bury my face in it.

Among other places.

I have one drink, she has two. I know that I can be a little intense at times, so I try to be relaxed so she can be comfortable.

"So, tell me about yourself, River?" she asks, tilting her head to the side as she studies me. A lock of her dark hair falls across her soft cheek, and I have to stop myself from gently pushing it away.

"What would you like to know?" I ask, arching my brow. Talking about myself isn't my strong suit. In fact, the less people know, the better. Which doesn't help much for dating, probably why I've done nothing but fuck around most of my life. Sex is easy. Letting someone know the real you? That shit is scary. I don't like to be vulnerable, and I don't like to have any weaknesses.

So I tell people what they want to hear. It works for me.

"Your connection to Romeo?" she asks, keeping her voice low.

"He's my cousin. Our mothers are sisters. You and Julianna?"

"Also cousins," she replies, plump lips kicking up at the corners. "On my mother's side."

"The famous all-girl curse," I say, referencing how the Angels are all females with no males being born to take on the MC's legacy.

"I'd say it's a blessing, not a curse. Too much testosterone and Lord knows what would happen," she teases.

I'm a member of the Devils Motorcycle Club and her family are the Angels. We're supposed to be enemies, but if I'm being honest, we've been peacefully coexisting since the Angels started. And the hierarchy within our clubs is similar to a monarchy, the presidency passing to the oldest male son of the president. Problem with the Angels is they have no male heirs, so it passes to the husband of the eldest daughter. For the Angels, that is Julianna.

And my dear cousin Romeo? He's the heir to the Devils. Hence the problem.

But Bella and I are just the cousins. Part of the court, so to speak.

"Why haven't I seen you around before?" I ask, studying her through narrowed eyes. I would have remembered.

She shrugs and takes a sip of her margarita. "I

work a lot and keep to myself. Plus we don't usually hang out on the same side of town as the Devils MC."

True. Vegas may seem small, but it's a pretty big area.

"Where do you work?" I ask, tapping my ring-covered fingers on the bar.

"I'm a property manager."

Of course she is. The Callistos are the masters of the local real estate industry, and own a lot of land and properties. They are never short on money.

"What about you?" she asks, giving me a once-over. "What do you do for the club?"

I wonder what she sees. Does she see the well-dressed, put-together guy, or the real man underneath?

The one with blood on his hands, and a dark soul.

After glancing down at my hands quickly, I look back up at her. "I'm Romeo's right-hand man" is all I say, smiling to distract her and then changing the subject. "Can I get you another drink, or something to eat?"

"I'm okay for now, thank you," she replies, licking the salt from her lips. "So you're the Devils version of Victor?"

I'm the Devils MC enforcer. I do whatever I need to. I'm not afraid to get my hands dirty, and most of the time I'd rather it be me than anyone else.

Why?

The shit that affects other people doesn't affect

me. I don't lose sleep over what I've had to do to earn my place in the club.

And I've heard about Victor, the man that's rumored to be taking over the Angels MC by marrying Julianna. He's not the man I'd want my future daughter marrying, that's for sure.

I laugh. "No, Bella. I am nothing like Victor."

She leans forward and smiles, then mouths the word *Good*.

Unable to stop myself, I lift my fingers to touch her cheek. "Do you want to get out of here?"

She arches her brow. "What have you got in mind?"

"I don't know. Let's go on an adventure. And don't worry, I will get you home safely. You can trust me."

I stand up and offer her my hand. She hesitates but takes it, and I lead her out of the bar and onto the back of my bike. It's not lost on me that she's the first woman I've ever let ride on the back of my bike, besides my sister. If my brother, Matthew, were here right now, he'd be giving me a lot of shit about it.

As we ride away, I feel a rush of adrenaline, and it has nothing to do with riding. Usually riding brings me a level of freedom that I can't get anywhere else. It's my church. It's where I exorcise my demons and repent for my sins. But with Bella's arms around me, it's a whole new experience.

She holds on to my leather jacket, and there is so much I want to know about her. But it's followed by a pang of sympathy. There's nothing good that I could give her or bring to her world.

I'm pain and torture and darkness. I can't show her that part of me. But I'm selfish enough to continue on.

I take her to my favorite place. It's a quiet hidden spot outside Vegas, near Lake Mead, with a stunning view. It's dark outside, but the moon on the lake gives us enough light to see where we are.

As I remove my jacket, then shirt, and start to undo my pants, her jaw drops open. "You're going in?"

I grin, flashing my teeth at her. "Yes, it's good for you. People do those ice baths all the time now—a little cold water isn't going to do anything."

She looks down at the water, her black heels so out of place. "What's in there?"

"Nothing that will hurt you," I reply, kicking off my leather boots and removing my jeans. "You better close your eyes right about now because I'm about to go in."

Instead of looking away, she boldly looks down at my cock, as if unable to help herself. I cover myself with my hands, smirking as I step into the water. It's cold, but not freezing.

It's refreshing.

I duck underneath and stand up and turn around to face her, only to hear some shuffling and a big splash as she jumps in.

Laughing, I wipe the water from my face and

lower myself so I'm covered up to my neck. She does the same. I can see her black bra straps, so I know she's not fully nude like myself.

"The water actually isn't too bad," she murmurs with a smile. "I haven't done anything like this since I was a kid."

Her makeup is running a little, but I've never seen a woman look more beautiful. I don't even know what it is about her. I don't really know her either. I was once upon a time sleeping with this spiritual woman, who told me about how sometimes you can be drawn to someone's energy, and aura.

I had no fucking idea what she was talking about.

Until now.

I'm *very* drawn to Bella.

There's a drop of water on her plump lips and I want to lick it off, but I don't want to scare her away. Instead I pull her closer to me. She laughs under her breath, and then says, "Race you to the other side," before diving underneath and disappearing into the abyss.

I appreciate the moment for a second, before diving in after her.

She wins, of course.

I lose track of how long we spend together in the lake, but when I get her out of the water she has the biggest smile on her face, and she looks so alive.

I'm happy I got to bring that out of her.

Or maybe she's always like this?

But at the end of the night when I drop her home, I

realize that she could win every little game between us, and I wouldn't care.

Because being with her would trump all of that.

Fuck.

Chapter One

Bella

Present

"You look even more beautiful pregnant," I tell my cousin Julianna, placing my hand on her small bump. I know some women don't like this, but Julianna told me I'm always welcome. She is so happy and in love with her husband, Romeo, and the two of them are the ultimate power couple, uniting the Angels and Devils motorcycle clubs and somehow running them both together. I don't know how they do it, but they make it work.

Sure, it hasn't been perfect. The Angels still stay in their clubhouse, and the Devils in theirs, but slowly the clubs are integrating. Julianna frequents both, making her new title as the first female president known in the MC world, with Romeo at her back.

They are perfect for each other.

I'm not one to compare relationships, but seeing where they are compared with where River and I are is a little depressing. River and I are still casually dating—exclusively, as far as I'm aware—but we are no way near as committed to each other as Julianna and Romeo.

To be fair, their courtship was fast. They went from meeting to married faster than a hockey season.

But River and me? Not anything more than just sleeping together, really.

In fact, I haven't even spoken to River in two days.

Two entire fucking days.

Now, I don't think of myself as a clingy person, but surely that is not normal.

He goes off and does his thing, and comes back to me when he's able to, or when he feels like it. At the start, it was good, because there was no pressure there, and after just turning down a proposal from my ex-boyfriend, Mark, I wasn't looking for anything serious. But then I met River, the sparks flew and I knew I didn't want to be with anyone else.

But River, he's a wild one.

He does what he wants, when he wants.

And it was so damn exciting at first.

But now it's been over a year, and we are still in the same place. He's still doing whatever he wants, but somehow that's starting to not work for me. I didn't want any pressure on the two of us, but after encouraging that we keep things casual, we haven't made any progress in our relationship. I still don't feel like I even really know him. He doesn't really bring me around his family, he hasn't met mine. We haven't even discussed living together or getting a dog. Nor have we discussed marriage and kids somewhere down the line.

Our mouths seem to be doing other things whenever we see each other.

"Thank you." Julianna beams over at me. She smooths down her floral dress and looks over her back garden. "I'm going to be honest, I feel so unprepared for this baby, like I have no idea what I'm doing. I'm just winging it."

"You'll be fine—you have me, and all of the MC to support you," I say.

She nods. "That's true. I don't know what I'd do without you all. How's everything with you? How's Sally working out in the office?"

Since Julianna stepped up as president of the Angels, she gave me the Callisto real estate empire to manage. Between her sisters, Rosalind and Veronica, who she isn't close with after the drama over the last few months, she couldn't trust anyone else not to sink the business. So we hired new staff and Sally is my new right-hand woman.

"She's good. Fast learner. Sweet," I answer honestly, while looking at the ten emails she's sent me since this morning. The girl is good, but she asks me a million questions, all in individual emails or texts.

"But…" Julianna fishes.

I sigh. "But she's not you."

Julianna smiles. "No one is me, but you need the help. I'll try to come in at least once a week until the baby arrives. I hear there are a few more properties coming in to purchase, including the infamous Lansdale property. I can't believe we finally got that one! I have been eyeing it for the last three years!"

"I know. I kept schmoozing with the seller's real estate agent—a little flirting never hurt—and out of the blue I got a call that they were ready to close. But it needs to happen within the week, or they will be going another direction."

"Good. That will put us way past our goals for the year. Have you vetted the sellers? The financials?"

"Yup, the Julianna Callisto system is in full effect." I give her a captain's salute.

She laughs. "Good. How's everything else?"

I take a sip of the soda she gave me, wondering how to answer this one. "Things in general are pretty good. Things with River, I don't know. I haven't even seen or heard from him in two days. Have you?"

She lifts her eyebrows. "Yeah, I saw him at the Devils clubhouse yesterday. He was running some errands for Romeo, I think. River is unpredictable, Bella. I did tell you this."

"I know," I agree on a sigh. I believe that she used the word *dangerous* when she was warning me. And he might be that, but never with me. "I think me and him need to have a conversation."

"Sounds like it." She nods, picking up and opening a jar of pickles and drinking the juice out of it, making me laugh. "I've been literally eating nothing but pickles for days now. I can't get enough of them, don't judge me."

"No judgment here," I reply, hiding my smirk. "I'm surprised you aren't eating them with the candy and sauce, like the viral challenge."

She pauses. "I haven't seen that. Whatever it is, I need it."

While she's searching *Chamoy pickle* on her phone, my mind wanders back to River. There's so much I still don't know about him, and I guess his mysteriousness drew me in at first. He's an enigma. I've never met a man like him before, and I think for the rest of the world that's probably a good thing. He's wild. Extremely intelligent. And charming.

What a dangerous mix.

Dangerous.

There's that word again.

I'd be lying if I say it doesn't excite me. I am in the Angels MC, after all.

But I'd also be lying if I say it doesn't scare the shit out of me. While I may have Angel MC in my blood, I'm not used to dating men like River. I know he's an enforcer, but I haven't really explored what that means, exactly. Ignorance is bliss and all.

Speak of the devil, his name pops up on my phone. "He's finally calling me."

Julianna takes the phone from me. "Let me answer. Hello?" she says, in the manliest voice she can muster, which isn't very convincing. Oh, shit. I cover my hand with my mouth. "Who am I? Who are you? Bella is busy."

She ends the call and turns to me. "See, now you won't have to wonder where he is anymore, because trust me, he's going to come looking for you."

I shake my head at her. "I can't believe you did that. He's going to be pissed."

She shrugs, unbothered. "Sometimes men need to have a little fear in them, or they get too comfortable and take you for granted. He shouldn't go missing for days on end without communicating with you." She pauses. "Unless you're into that. I could see the benefits."

"Well, this is going to be interesting," I murmur, smirking. "He's not even calling back."

She laughs. "Nah, he'll be climbing on his bike right now, trust me. And since you're not at home, then he's going to get even angrier."

Fifteen minutes pass before Julianna's phone rings.

"Yes?" she says, sounding sweet as ever.

"Where's Bella? She's not at home," I can hear River growl.

She looks over at me with wide eyes, and I shrug. This is her game—she can play it as she sees fit. I'm finding the whole thing amusing, because I doubt anyone plays with River like this.

No one would have the balls.

"What's that? You're cutting out," she says, making some static noise with her mouth, and then presses End Call.

"Brutal," I say, amused. "Being pregnant has brought out your villain era, and I'm here for it."

She laughs, rubbing her belly. "I do feel a little untouchable right now. But also quite vulnerable. It's weird. Like I'm strong but weak at the same time. I'm growing a person inside of me, but if someone chased me, I probably wouldn't make it very far."

"No one would get close enough to you even if they were trying to chase after you," I muse, reaching for a carrot stick on the platter in front of me. "You'd have two MCs jumping in between. Trust me, you're the safest woman on the earth."

"So are you," she replies, reaching out and taking my hand. "River would do anything to protect you. And his anything would have no limits."

We share a smile, but it drops the second we hear a motorcycle ride into the driveway.

"That's him." I'd know the sound of his bike anywhere.

"Ever the protector." Julianna glances around and wrinkles her nose. "Wait, you guys aren't going to have sex out here, are you?" She stands up and smirks. "I can go hide in my room."

I roll my eyes at her. "We are not having sex at your house!"

She laughs and moves to head inside. "Guess I better let the beast inside."

"I'll get it, he's my beast," I mutter in a dry tone. "You sit and relax."

She leans back into her seat and picks up her drink. Which of course happens to be pickle juice. "Good luck."

After closing the sliding door behind me, I go the front door and open it, coming face-to-face with the man I've fallen in love with. He's in all-black leather, his gloves still on, his hand still up in the air ready to knock again. Blue eyes the color of the ocean narrow, and the air around him is thick. He's angry, but he's controlling himself.

"What game are you playing, Bella?" he asks, teeth clenched. He pulls me against his cut and lifts my face up to him, cupping my cheek a little rougher than necessary.

"It wasn't me, it was—"

He lifts me up and throws me over his shoulder. "Julianna, we're going! Romeo is on his way home now!"

"Okay, bye," she calls back, her amused voice getting closer as she locks the door behind us.

And then I'm placed on the back of his bike, a helmet slid on my head. I hold on to him as he starts the engine, and then takes off without a word.

His body is tense, but you know what?

The conversation we're about to have has been a long time coming.

But I'm more than ready for it.

And even though he's angry as fuck at me, he still

reaches back to rest the heel of his palm on my thigh when we stop at the lights.

And that's just one reason I'm fighting for us.

Chapter Two

River

Most people know better than to push me.

I'd never do anything to hurt Bella, but I'm not going to lie, the anger and jealousy that raged through me has been unexpected. I should have known better. Bella isn't the type to cheat, but when someone else picked up her phone, I just saw red.

Yes, I know I'm not being rational. It was Julianna. But the surprise of it caught me off guard.

Bella is mine.

I don't know why she thought it was a good idea to test me, but I'm going to find out momentarily. I've been busy the last few days. My new dual role as vice president and enforcer for the Devils MC is being put to the test as I help Romeo navigate his own new spot as president. I'm his right-hand man, his muscle and his go-to whenever he needs a problem fixed and kept silent. But that doesn't mean I don't think about Bella or want to be with her. And it doesn't mean that I don't keep her safe, because I have men drive by her house every damn night to check on her if I'm not around.

The second we stop at the Devils clubhouse, I get off, and as soon as she removes the helmet, I pick her up once more and all but run inside with her.

"You know I can walk, right?" she yells, slapping at my back.

"Yeah, I know you can answer your phone properly, too," I reply sarcastically.

I just rented out my property, so the clubhouse is now my permanent residence. Looks like she's going to have to try to be quiet.

Or let everyone hear, I don't give a fuck.

But either way, she's about to be screaming my name.

I ignore everyone I see on the way, close my bedroom door behind us and gently throw her on the bed. She bounces on the mattress a few times while staring daggers at me.

"What is your problem?" she asks, but seriously, she knows exactly what my problem is. She created it.

"Well, you obviously wanted my attention, so now you have it," I growl, crossing my arms over my chest. My teeth are clenched, but I'm trying my best to not scare her. My mother was always scared of my father, and I could never do that to the woman I want to be with. I couldn't bear it if she was scared of me, but at the same time she obviously wanted to provoke me.

I need someone who can give it right back to me and know that I would never harm her. Bella has never seen me truly angry, and I'd like to keep it that way.

She stands up and copies my body language. Okay, she's definitely not scared, and I like that. I feel myself harden even further at her confident stare. "I haven't heard from you in two days, so apparently that's what I have to do to get some attention around here."

"And there we have it," I say under my breath. I pull my riding gloves off, and then sit down and take off my black leather boots. All the while I can feel her anger building in the silence.

"That's all you have to say? 'And there we have it'? And there we have what, River? We've been together for over a year now. Don't you think we need to take it a little more seriously? You could at least send me a text message, let me know you're okay, and when you'll find the time to see me—"

I shut her up by standing again, pushing her against the closed door and kissing her. She kisses me back, but I can taste her anger. And I know she's not asking for anything unreasonable.

But fuck.

I've never had to answer to anyone in my life.

She bites my lip and then pushes me away. "You

do not get to get out of this conversation by going all alpha and kissing me."

"What if I postpone the conversation?" I say, my face right near hers. Our bodies are pressed against each other so close, my weight is pinning her to the door.

I don't move to kiss her, instead waiting for her to make the first move. I need her to do it. As we stand there panting for a few beats, she says, "We're having this goddamn conversation, but after you get me off," and pulls me to her.

Our kiss isn't sweet. Instead of having a fight with our words, our mouths are doing a different kind of battle. She moves back, breaking the kiss, and reaches down for my belt, undoing it without breaking eye contact. She's so beautiful, especially when she's mad, her gray eyes like the ash from a raging fire.

What happens when fire meets iron?

Someone must bend, waver to the other, and it's not going to be me.

I carry her to the bed, strip her down until she's in nothing but her black panties, and then slowly remove the rest of my clothing while staring down at her. She does the same with her panties. Her chest lifts with every deep breath, the tension between us filling the room, and making the air thick with desire.

Now that we're both naked, I kneel on the bed and stare down at her, admiring her body. She is perfect. I wonder if she knows just how much.

She gets impatient and sits up, all but jumping on me and kissing me, pressing her body against mine and wrapping her hands around my nape. I hold on to the globes of her ass and lift her so she's sitting on my lap, and she wraps her legs around me. I can feel her wetness, and it makes me even harder.

"Make me feel good," she says, and I push back down on the bed and prepare to feast on her. She lies back, giving me her fuck-me eyes, and I lick my way down her body. I've never been hungrier for her, and after she comes three times, she stops me from giving her more.

"Have me," she says into my ear after pulling me to her, digging her nails into my back, so I give her what she wants and slide my cock inside her. Slowly at first, and then she turns over and starts to ride me hard and fast, while I hold on for dear life and try not to tumble backward off the bed and onto the floor. My head falls back, and she kisses my neck, biting and sucking, and I don't even care if she leaves a mark on me.

When we're about to fall off the mattress, I push her back on the bed, still inside her, and fuck her hard, just how she likes it, hitting that sweet spot until she's moaning and saying my name. I put her legs on my shoulders and go inside so deep, and when she comes, her thighs trembling as wave after wave of pleasure hits, I can't help but follow suit, looking into her eyes. I love that she gives me eye contact right back, never getting too intense for her.

I gently remove her legs back down and stroke her face, kissing her lips, until I roll off her.

We lie side by side afterward, still naked, but no longer angry. I know that communication isn't my strongest skill, nor is being vulnerable, but if I want this woman, I have to listen to her and make her happy. If that means sending her a fucking message telling her what I'm up to, then so be it. If I want to keep her in my life, I need to be able to compromise, and become the man that she wants me to be. I've never been in a serious relationship before, so I know that it's going to mean some change for me. I need to stop being so stuck in my ways and let her in.

And for her, I think I can do that.

"I'll do better," I say, reaching out and tucking her hair back behind her ear. "And text and call you to let you know what I'm up to."

To some extent, anyway. Most of the time she wouldn't want to know what I'm up to, because she's a good person and has morals, unlike me. I'd never want her to know the things I've done and the things I'm capable of doing. She would probably never want to see me again.

"Okay," she says, a small smile playing on her lips. "That wasn't so hard, was it?"

For a normal person, no, that wouldn't be.

And I might act relaxed on the outside, funny even, but underneath and inside my head it's a whole different story. I'm complicated, dark and not used to letting people in.

"I've never had a proper relationship," I admit, kissing her forehead. "So you're going to have to be a little patient with me."

Any women I've slept with has been casual and pretty one-sided, with me in control of when and where I saw them. There were no emotions involved, just lust and desire. This. This is something different.

Which can make it a little fucking scary at times.

I'm completely out of my comfort zone, because I really do care.

And it makes it hard.

And let's be honest, I didn't grow up seeing a happy marriage between my parents. And sometimes that makes me not trust myself. I keep saying I'm nothing like my father, but at the end of the day that was all I knew and saw. He was a monster, and the apple never falls far from the tree. At least that's what they say.

Sometimes I wish better for Bella, but I'm too fucking selfish to let her walk away.

"River, I've been nothing but patient," she says, running her red fingernails over my bicep. "But we're together, and I know you are used to doing your own thing, but you have me to consider, too."

I imagine her watching Julianna get married and now pregnant probably has her reexamining our relationship, which is still pretty casual. We haven't moved forward at all since we first started dating, although we did become exclusive with each other, without ever discussing it.

I really do suck at all of this.

"You're right," I reply, swallowing hard. I roll her onto her back and lie on top of her, my hard cock pressing against her. "But don't try to make me jealous again, because if you were with another man, it wouldn't have ended well for him."

She has the nerve to smirk. "That was Julianna."

"You didn't stop her."

She shrugs, amusement dancing in her eyes. "I wanted to see how it played out."

"You knew how it would play out," I reply, nuzzling her neck and gently biting her soft skin. "You are mine, but apparently you like to be reminded of that."

"I do when I haven't heard from you in two days," she replies, sighing in pleasure as I kiss her jawline. "But you've obviously heard me."

"Loud and clear," I say, and then slide back into her.

"Good, then hopefully we won't have another misunderstanding like this again. But River… I can't wait forever. I know you need to go slow, but there are things I want from life and I need to know if you and I could do those things together. And if you can't…"

I stop her with a kiss. This is getting too serious, too real. She doesn't even know who I really am. I'm not ready to deal with that right now. The physical part has never been hard for us, pun not intended. We could fuck all day and night, and if I could be with her all the time, then I would. This is the first time

I've brought her back to the Devils clubhouse, and I guess doing that makes it pretty fucking official. The men are only just getting used to having Julianna there full-time, so I didn't want to push them any further until they're ready.

Last thing they need to think is that the Angels are taking over our clubhouse. But it's not my fault their women are so fucking sexy, and this one has had me enthralled from the moment I laid eyes on her. So now they know. And I hope to bring her here more often. Things will need to change if I want to truly fit her into my life, and that means trusting that she will maybe accept me once she gets to know me.

Maybe that's asking too much, I know.

My phone starts ringing, but I ignore it.

And then I show her once more who she belongs to.

Chapter Three

Bella

As usual, Romeo keeps calling River at the worst time, so as soon as we've had a shower together, he leaves me alone in his room.

His room that I've never even seen until now. River has always met me at my place, which has more privacy. A few men saw me being carried into their clubhouse, so I know they're probably all gossiping about it as we speak. Whoever said women gossip more than men have never been to a clubhouse of bikers. There are no secrets here, and everyone knows everyone's business.

I get dressed and then have a look around his room while I'm in here alone, because what else would I do? It doesn't seem like he has many belongings. The wooden California king bed takes up the center of the space. There's a massive television mounted on the wall and mirrored sliding doors conceal his closet. The dark curtains and bedsheets give it almost a cabin-like feel. There are no photos or little knickknacks or anything like that, nothing really personalized. I slide open the mirror and touch his rack of clothing, all in black or denim, and eye his stash of weapons all perfectly placed and organized. He clearly likes things neat and tidy.

I jump out of my skin as the door opens and I wince at being caught red-handed snooping through his shit, but it's not River standing there. Instead, it's a beautiful young woman with red hair, freckles and a knowing smirk.

"Don't worry, if I were you, I'd be doing the exact same," she says, lip twitching. Her hazel eyes are warm, yet somehow sad.

I slide the door shut, clearing my throat. "I don't know what you mean." We both laugh at my outright lie.

"I'm Corey," she introduces, offering me her hand. "River's sister. He told me to come and keep you company while he's helping Romeo contain some kind of disaster, no doubt. Can I get you something to drink or eat?"

I smile. "I'm Bella, and yes, I'd love something to drink."

"I know who you are," she replies, beckoning me to follow her out. "We've all heard about River's woman, but none of us have met you in person besides Romeo, and, of course, Julianna. The men were questioning if you even existed." She pauses. "I mean, not to River's face, anyway."

I laugh and follow her out into the hallway, and then through to the kitchen where she opens the fridge wide. "Okay, we have beer, juice, soda…"

"I'll have a soda, please."

She pulls out two colas and hands me one. In the natural light, her hazel eyes are stunning. She looks nothing like River, but I wonder what it's been like growing up with him as her brother.

"You are very pretty," she blurts out.

"Funny, I was just thinking the same about you," I say, grinning.

A man wearing leather sticks his head in the room. "You're River's woman?"

I nod, lip twitching.

"How the hell did he get you? You're fucking hot." He winces. "But don't tell him I said that."

Corey arches her brow and nods toward the man. "That's Jeremiah. He clearly has no manners."

He smiles widely, flashing his straight white teeth. "Nice to meet you."

"You, too," I reply, looking between them both. All I'm hearing from them is a whole lot of "don't tell River" comments, which means they must not want to upset him or get on his bad side. What exactly is his bad side? "And don't worry, I won't tell River that you think I'm fucking hot, or that you all questioned whether I even existed to begin with."

"That would be wonderful," Jeremiah says, smirking. He runs a hand through his light, almost white-blond hair and turns his green eyes to Corey. "Get me a beer, would you?"

"Get it yourself," she responds, her cheerful tone contradicting her words.

He sighs and does just that, while Corey and I take a seat at the dining table.

"What are the men in the Angels MC like?" she asks, a contemplative expression on her face. "I mean, I know the MCs are considered one now, but I still don't see many of the men. It's not like they're walking into our clubhouse unless there's a party going on or something."

"Why do you want to know? You want to be matched up?" I ask, amusement in my tone. I open the cap of the soda and take a sip.

Jeremiah makes a choking sound. "Yeah, maybe don't do that. Unless you want River to kill one of them."

Corey rolls her eyes. "Do you see what I have to deal with? I can't even talk about dating someone around here. Maybe the Angels will be different."

"They won't be. They are still men, and bikers," he comments.

"So you don't want to be hooked up, then," I tease, smirking.

Okay, so River is very protective of his sister. Knowing him, I'm not surprised at all. He's the exact same with me. And I can understand why, especially in the world we live in. Men take advantage if they can, and seem to have the upper hand and all the power. That's why I love that Julianna has stepped up to lead us. Yes, alongside Romeo, but she's the one I'd go to if I had a problem. She's strong and capable and has Romeo at her back.

And I'm here for it.

"No, I just want to know if all bikers are the same, I guess," Corey grumbles, bringing me back to the conversation. Jeremiah leaves the kitchen with a handful of beers.

"I don't think so. I've never met anyone like River before," I admit with a fond smile.

Yeah, he can be a lot. But he's mine, and I love every second of being with him.

Her eyes widen. "I don't know if the world could handle more than one River. I love him, I do, but he's…" She trails off, studying me. "How did you get him to commit to you? You must be very good in bed."

I choke on my drink.

"I just mean you tamed the beast, somehow. He's never openly dated anyone that I've seen. So you must be very special," she corrects, blushing. "Sometimes I say things without thinking."

A gentle smile escapes me. Julianna told me about Corey, and how she and River lost their other brother, Matthew, at the hands of the Angels MC, before the Angels and the Devils MC united. It's nice to see that she's joking and smiling, because Julianna said she was in a dark place as she was grieving the loss. I know River was grieving, too; he just happens to hide it a lot better, along with everything else. He doesn't like to show any weakness.

"Well, I like your lack of filter," I reply, winking at her. "I wish that everyone just said what they were thinking."

Her eyes flash. "Yeah, I don't know about that. People don't want to know some things. It makes them uncomfortable."

I notice her fiddling with the cuff of her cardigan, and my eyes are drawn to her wrist. She pulls the material up to her palm, but I still get a glimpse of the scars there. At some point, or even now, she's been cutting herself. I want to reach out to her and comfort her, but I don't know how well she'd take that from a stranger.

"The right people will want to know all the things, the light and the dark," I say, smiling sadly at her. "Especially the dark, because that's when you need your friends and family the most."

She nods slowly, a contemplative expression on her face. "You're very nice, Bella."

"Thank you."

"Can I give you some advice?" she asks, staring straight into my soul.

"Um…sure?"

She doesn't blink. "Run. If you're smart, you will run."

She then gets up and leaves me alone in the kitchen. Wow, that went from friendly to intense. I've been dating River for almost a year, but why am I only now picking up on the signs everyone has been throwing at me? What is it about River that has people on edge? And why don't I see that side of him? I think I need to start asking better questions when it comes to him.

I sip my soda and consider heeding her advice, but then River comes in, smiling warmly when he finds me. "There you are." Bending down, he kisses me quickly and pulls me up to him. "Where's Corey?"

"She left a minute ago," I say, going up on my tip-toes and wrapping my arms around him. "I should get home."

"I'll come over tonight around ten," he says, eyes dancing with amusement. "See, you can teach an old dog new tricks."

"I'm glad," I reply in a dry tone, shaking my head at him. But it's nice for him to let me know what his plans are, and not leave me wondering when his ass is going to show up next.

He gives me a ride home, kisses me deeply and waits for me to safely get inside before he disappears to do biker man things.

"Hello, Hades," I say in a baby voice as my dog runs up and jumps on me. "I missed you, too." He's getting older now, but he's still my best friend and a wonderful guard dog. He's never been that bright, but we can't have it all, can we? He has his big Staffy smile on and it melts my heart. "Come on, you can help me with the gardening."

After Covid hit, I started my own vegetable garden so if the world ever goes to shit, I have my own food right here. I went from someone who has never even owned a plant, to someone with beautiful indoor plants and a jungle in her garden, mostly native species. It's a challenge finding what vegetables grow best when, and I enjoy being kept on my toes. I fill a basket up with lettuce, tomato, cucumbers and celery, planning on using it to make a salad for tonight. I'm washing my hands in the sink when there's a knock at the door.

Frowning, as I'm not expecting anyone, I peep through the hole and see none other than Mark standing there.

My ex-boyfriend Mark.

All-American, brown hair, brown eyes, athletic build. He was perfect. Until he wasn't.

We dated for a year and broke up a few months before I met River, when Mark proposed but I didn't feel ready. I knew I had to end it with him when I realized I would never feel ready, because he wasn't the right person for me. I could never see myself growing old or having children with him.

Ever since then he has shown up sporadically, frequenting places he knows I love, calling and texting, and now for the first time just simply showing up at my front door.

I don't know what to do.

Did someone we mutually know die or something? Maybe his mom is sick and he wants to tell me. Not that I've met his mom yet.

Get a grip on yourself, Bella. He isn't an axe murderer. You know him.

I open the door slowly, deciding to face him. "Mark, hey. What are you doing here?" I ask. Friendly but formal, those are the vibes I'm going for here.

"Hey, Bella," he says, smiling widely and showing off his perfect veneers. "Sorry to just drop in, but I was in the neighborhood and thought I would be spontaneous and see if you were interested in having coffee or something?" When we broke up, I told him that we never do anything spontaneous, and he's obviously held on to that.

"Oh, um." I shift on my feet, trying to think of a legitimate excuse that will let him down gently. Instead, I take advice from Corey and just say exactly what I'm thinking. "That's very nice of you, but I'm actually dating someone and I don't think it's appropriate to hang out with my ex-boyfriend. I think you need to move on and find someone who is a perfect fit for you."

He lifts up his hand. "Actually, I just got married and wanted to let you know in person before you heard it from someone else."

Awkward.

"That is awesome, congratulations. But I don't think that required a home visit," I reply, wincing. "I wish you nothing but happiness."

"Bella, wait," he says, before I can close the door. "I just want to have a chat."

I hesitate, not wanting to invite him in, but also

not wanting to be rude. But at the end of the day, I don't feel like he would act inappropriately, so I let my manners win out.

"Okay," I reply, opening the door and letting him inside.

He sits down on the couch as he glances around my place. "Been a while since I was here."

"Yes, it has." Because we broke up. Who wants to engage in a conversation with their ex? Or have them show up unannounced?

Not me.

No one sane would.

Not that I have anything against him, but he's my past, and I don't want to look back. I have no reason to.

"So what did you want to talk about?" I ask, studying him. He's a good-looking man, but I don't feel anything for him. Not even a smidge of attraction.

"I guess I just wanted some…closure, you know? I thought we were going well, and then I asked you to marry me and you kind of ran off," he says, shrugging.

He wants closure, after he has already married someone else?

How odd.

"Well, I just think we weren't right for each other, and you are obviously happily married now, so…" I say, forcing a smile.

"Yeah, you're right. I'm sorry. Coming here was a bad idea. I think I just wanted to know if there was anything I did specifically so that I can make sure not to be that way with my wife."

I smile. Mark is a good guy. He never did anything wrong, never treated me wrong. I think I've been around bikers too long. I'm cynical and expect everyone to be like Victor, the man who Julianna was meant to marry, who turned out to be a monster. He went power hungry and subsequently "disappeared" after he killed Matthew, River and Corey's brother.

"It wasn't you, Mark. I just don't think we were compatible in the long run."

"But we dated for a year. I thought we were on the right path."

As he says that, I realize he was in the same situation I am in with River. We've been together for a year, and I thought everything had been okay, up until it hit me that we are stuck in the same place. What does this mean? Does that mean River doesn't see a future with me? Is that why we've been moving so slow?

As I'm having my mini freak-out, I realize Mark is waiting for a response, and for the first time, I feel like I really do owe him an explanation.

"Mark, we were great. And I thought we wanted the same things. But when you proposed, our life flashed before my eyes, and it just wasn't what I saw for myself. I'm so sorry. I don't think I realized you were more serious about the relationship than I was until that moment, and I do feel horrible."

Mark nods and smiles. "Thank you. I think I've been holding on to…something. And that is really helpful for me to hear. I appreciate you saying this to me."

We make small talk for another ten minutes, and I ask about his wife and their wedding. I find that I do miss the easy conversation he and I used to have. He uses the bathroom before getting up to leave.

"This was nice. Thank you for stopping by," I say, and mean it.

"Maybe we can actually be friends," he says with a wave before going to his car.

When he's gone, I close the door and lean back on it, trying not to imagine that I'm Mark in my current situation.

And then I get a text from River.

River: Who the fuck was that at your door?

Brow furrowing, I glance around trying to figure out how the fuck he would know that.

Bella: Where are you?

River: At the clubhouse. Now answer my question.

Bella: Not until you explain.

River: I have someone drive around now and again to make sure you're all right.

That is both cute and kind of invasive.

Bella: You have no boundaries, do you?

River: Can never be too careful in our world.

Bella: I have cameras.

I consider myself an independent woman, but I'm also not an idiot. This world of ours is dangerous, and you always have to be prepared. Especially after everything that happened with Julianna last year.

River: I can't see the stream.

I roll my eyes.

Bella: Connect yourself to them. I know you've thought about it if you haven't done it already.

River: I did want to.

Bella: You have my permission.

River: You didn't answer me.

Bella: Was an ex-boyfriend. Came to tell me that he's married.

River: He comes back and I'm taking care of him.

Bella: How?

River: Depends on my mood.

If he can use my security cameras, it will save them some manpower having someone driving around here doing boundary checks. He's overbearing, but at the same time I've never felt safer.

And in a motorcycle club, that is worth more than gold.

Chapter Four

River

My mother, Lisa, lives about an hour away from the clubhouse, and I try to make it out there at least once a week. I know I should probably visit her more, but it's not always easy to get away, and I have to make sure that no one is following me.

My mother has had a hard life, and it makes me happy to know that the rest of her days will be peaceful. I bought her a town house and pay all of her bills, so she never wants for anything. She volunteers in an animal refuge and spends her time looking after them and drinking coffee in her garden.

And as for my father, well, we don't talk about him.

"River!" She beams when she opens the door. She's wearing a patch over her right eye, the one that she lost sight in years ago. "Come inside. You have to see the foster kittens I have right now."

She takes my arm and leads me to the lounge room,

where four little ginger kittens are playing. "Look how cute they are."

I sit down and place one in my lap. "They are pretty damn adorable."

"Do you want something to drink? Coffee?"

"Sure," I reply, petting another kitten that tries to climb up my jean-clad leg.

We have coffee together, and she tells me about her week. I don't really tell her about mine, and she doesn't press.

"How's Bella?" she asks, her one visible green eye filled with curiosity. Ever since I told her I met someone, she always asks about her. I know I should bring Bella here to meet her, but I've been keeping this side of my life separate. I love my mom, but Bella would have questions that I don't want to answer about my childhood, and my father. I'm not ready to have that conversation, especially with Matthew gone, too. My family is full of sadness, and I just don't want to bring that to Bella.

"She's good," I say, smiling at the mere mention of her. "She told me I need to act like more of a boyfriend and tell her where I am and when I'm going to see her."

Mom laughs. "That's more than fair, River. I'm glad she's speaking up and telling you what she needs from you. I'd like to meet her."

"I know, I'll have to bring her sometime," I say, before changing the subject. "Is there anything you need done around the house? Anything I can help with?" Last time I upgraded her security system, and the time before that I fixed her fence so her foster dogs couldn't get out.

"Actually, yes," she says, perking up. "My chain saw stopped working on me yesterday. Would you mind looking at it?"

"Of course," I say. "And next week I'll bring some extra firewood for you, too. We should start stocking up for winter."

I fix the chain saw, cut some wood for her and then take her out for an early dinner. I don't like that she's so far away, but she has a lot of friends here, and this is where she wanted to retire. People still stare at her eye patch, but it doesn't seem to bother her. She's a brave woman, my mother.

After we finish our meals and she has a strawberry mojito, I drop her home and head home for a shower before going to Bella's house.

It's dark when I get there, but earlier than I had told her. She answers the door in her robe, freshly showered and a beautiful smile on her face.

"Have you eaten?" she asks before anything else.

"I have, have you? I can get you something if you want," I offer, gazing down at the curve of her breast, the pink silk wrapped around it tightly. "Unless you are hungry for something else? Then I don't need to go anywhere."

She rolls her eyes. "I just ate. I saved you a plate in case you hadn't had anything yet."

I cup her face. "You are so sweet, you know that?"

And then she drags me into her bedroom and thanks me for being such a good boy, with her hands, her mouth and then her pussy on my face.

The next night, blood drips from my knuckles. I lift the man in front of me by his shirt. "Who sent you?"

I noticed someone following Romeo and me early this morning, and when I saw the same car again just now, I knew it wasn't a coincidence. It's my job to stay vigilant and protect Romeo and the MC, and I'm not going to let this slide until I find out why this man is snooping around and how much of a threat he is.

The driver spits out blood on the alleyway. "I already said I don't know what you're talking about. I have no fucking idea who you are."

He's lying.

I know it, he knows it, which means unfortunately for him I'm not done yet.

He's either brave or stupid, and I don't care which one it is, because I'm going to find out what information I need from him regardless.

I slam him back against the wall and look him in the eyes. "We can do this the easy way or the hard way."

"I don't know—"

"The fuck you don't," I growl, bringing my face closer. "I want to know what you want, and why you are following us."

This time he spits in my face, and that's when I really lose my temper.

I wipe my face and then hit him hard enough to knock him out, and throw him in the trunk of my car and head back to the clubhouse. I then send a text to Romeo asking for him to send someone out to get the man's car.

There's one thing I've learned during my time on earth, and that is to trust my gut instincts, because they have never let me down before. This man is not a friend, and I'm going to find out what he wants.

I park in the clubhouse garage, and Jeremiah and Romeo are waiting for me.

"Well, this escalated," Jeremiah says, whistling as he opens the trunk. "He's out cold."

"Always escalates with River." Romeo smirks. He lays the man down on the ground and searches him, pulling out his wallet and checking the man's ID.

"This is fake," he says, throwing it down next to the unconscious body.

We all share a look. We are under the impression that the threats have been eliminated since the Angels and Devils joined.

So the question is, who else is out to get us?

We search his car and run the plate numbers before we hide the vehicle. Nothing. Stolen car. Fake ID. We have nothing on this guy, but all I know is that he won't be going anywhere until we figure this out.

I tie him up and he wakes up right away when I move him. "You ready to do some talking?"

"Fuck you." He sneers, trying to get out of his

binds. I pick him up and set him back against the garage wall. "You can't just keep me here!"

Romeo and Jeremiah both look at me and then head back inside the clubhouse, leaving me alone with our new guest. I pull out and slowly unroll my torture kit, and press a button so the garage door scrolls down, slowly shutting out the light…

And all hope.

Chapter Five

Bella

As I'm about to leave work and go home for the evening after a long day of meeting with real estate
agents, I find myself wondering what River is up to
right now. We definitely spend our days very differently. My job is consistent and stable, yet River's job
seems anything but that. He could be doing random
things at any given time, from working at one of the
businesses, to hiding a body. I mean, I wouldn't really know, because I don't hear the minor details,
but I can guess.

I guess opposites really do attract,

For me, becoming a property manager was a no-
brainer as a Callisto—it kind of comes with the ter-
ritory and family name. Property and motorcycles
are our thing, and I know which one I'm more comfortable with. As much as I love riding on the back
of a bike, I never got into riding them myself.

Bella: You coming over tonight? I can make us dinner.

I send River a quick text about potentially coming over for a home-cooked meal tonight as I get in my black BMW, and stop at the store to grab some groceries before heading home. From the outside, I don't think anyone would know I was a part of an MC family. I probably look like any other business-woman, in my white blouse and beige tailored slacks. But how different my life is. I suppose, unlike Julianna, I got to live my life with one foot out the door, and without all the responsibilities that she has.

But now being with River, who is so heavily tied into the MC, I have both feet firmly planted in one direction, and that is wherever he is. I haven't given myself much time to process this, which is probably why I let River off the hook so easily. While this relationship is still very firmly in the casual phase, he's not the only reason it is. I never pictured myself dating a biker, let alone marrying one. No judgment to my family or Julianna, but the biker life was never for me. I wanted "normal," or what I saw on television.

But as Julianna quickly found out, the heart wants what the heart wants. Yeah, yeah, Selena Gomez, you were right.

While Mark was not the one I ever imagined being with for the long term, he's the type of guy I saw myself ending up with. Normal guy with a normal job.

I think he was an accountant or something. I actually don't remember what he did other than he went to work in a suit every day. Shit, I was not a great girlfriend.

As I'm pondering my life, my assistant, Sally, calls. "Hey," I answer while pulling into my driveway.

"Bella, I'm so glad I caught you. I was finishing up at the office working on the Lansdale property you gave me to finalize. There's quite a bit of information missing that we normally need for me to enter into the system. Do you happen to have that info handy? It also needs your signature."

Shit. The Lansdale property was something Julianna told me I needed to handle. I must not have properly looked over all the paperwork before I gave it to Sally.

"I'm sorry, Sally, I didn't realize so much was missing. Is there a deadline to close?" As I wait for her response, I pull out my notebook to take a look at my notes. Shit, I left that at the office.

"End of day tomorrow."

Dammit. "Okay, I'll handle it first thing tomorrow morning."

As I hang up, I get a text from River.

River: Can't tonight, sorry. Tomorrow?

Bella: Sounds good.

At least he's actually communicating with me now, and doesn't just go MIA with no explanation.

The next day I decide to show up at the clubhouse before I head into the office with some food for him. This is the first time I've come here unannounced, but I figure Julianna might be around also.

Jeremiah arches his brow and looks up from his Fitbit when he sees me. He must have gone for a run—he's bare chested, a sheen of sweat covering his six-pack abs. He's a good-looking man, I'm not going to lie. With that light hair and his green eyes, he kind of looks ethereal. But the clothes he usually wears don't make him look like an angel. He likes black and leather. Even now, his running shorts and sneakers are black.

"Hey, Bella, what are you doing here?" he asks, taking his earbuds out. "Does River know you're here?" His tone makes me feel like now might not be the best time for me to be here.

I shift my feet in my black block heels, wondering if I should turn around now. "No, I was just dropping off some food for him. Is that okay?"

That seems to distract him, as he looks at what's in my hands. "Is there any food in there for me? Because I am starving."

"Yeah," I laugh, looking down at the bag in my hands. "I put a lot in there. There will be plenty." Knowing that the other men would likely want some, it would be rude for me to bring something just for River, and not for the others.

Jeremiah grins, flashing his teeth. "Well, why didn't you say so? Come on in."

Shaking my head in amusement, I follow behind him, wondering why he was giving me the vibe like now isn't a good time to be here. Is something going on? Should I turn around and leave? This is River's home and I want to get comfortable here, but only if I'm wanted.

Surprising him wasn't the best idea. I kind of knew that. River is mysterious and likes to be in control. I doubt he'd appreciate me coming here on my own accord. But how are we ever going to cross this line and get closer if we don't step out of our comfort zones? I want us to progress in our relationship, and guess what, these are the type of things people in a relationship do. I'm not doing anything out of the ordinary. Although it might feel that way for him, because he doesn't seem used to having a normal, open connection with someone. I don't want to push him, though, because it might make him step backward from me.

Why are men so complicated?

River is a whole different ball game of dating.

"Maybe I should come back another time? If he's busy." But I don't really want to do that, do I?

"You're here now," Jeremiah says, shrugging. He leads me to the kitchen, and I place the food on the table and open the containers filled with eggs, bacon and potatoes.

"Help yourself," I say, forcing a smile. I look around the kitchen, wondering what I should do next. Should I just leave now?

Jeremiah starts loading his plate. What he doesn't do is go and get River, or tell me where to find him. "This looks pretty fucking good," he murmurs, doing a little dance.

I smirk. "What was that?"

"This?" he asks, doing the dance again.

"Yes, that."

"That's my happy food dance. You know, when something looks delicious and you're happy you're about to eat it. You don't have one?" he asks, sounding surprised. "I thought everyone had one."

I try to hide my smile. That's kind of cute.

When he starts to heat up the food, I decide to go and check myself if River is in his room. He isn't, and nothing but a perfectly made bed looks back at me. I close the door and walk past the empty gym, then turn around. This was an epic waste of time. And I don't even know if River is here.

Bella: Where are you?

I'm about to call it quits when I hear his voice say, "Romeo, where are you?"

I know I should just go, but I'm nosy and I want to

see my man. He never tells me what he's up to with the club, and I usually never ask, but that doesn't mean that I'm not curious, because trust me, I am.

I place my hand on the knob that opens the door to what I assume is the garage and turn it. It's dark in there, but not too dark for me to take in what is right in front of me.

Sitting in a chair is a man who is bound and bloodied. A figure is standing above him, pummeling him over and over.

"River?" I call out, more on instinct. Asking him to save me from the sight I'm witnessing. But what I see surprises me. At the sound of my voice, the figure turns, then rushes over to me, pushing me out of the garage, and closing the door behind me.

It is River.

"Bella? What the fuck are you doing here?" he growls, hands shaking as they touch my arms. He scans my eyes intently, and I can see how angry he is. But I also see a little flash of fear in those beautiful blue eyes, too.

I'm stunned speechless after taking in what I saw. Or rather what I didn't see. I'm not naive. I know that violence is part of these MCs, but... But I never expected to be sleeping with the man who actually does that part. Okay, but I knew he was the enforcer. I guess thinking something and seeing it firsthand are two different things. River, my beautiful, dark hero.

I find it hard to reconcile the person I know with the person I saw in the garage.

I realize I'm just gawking at him, so I say the first thing that comes out of my mouth.

"I brought you some food," I say, clearing my throat. "And then I wanted to see you and say hello before I go to work."

He backs me up against the hallway wall and stares down at me. There's a menacing look to him. I'm not afraid. I know he won't hurt me. But it's definitely not a look I've seen him have before. "There's a lot going on here—that's why I couldn't come over last night. And it's why you shouldn't be here right now."

"What *are* you doing in there?" I ask. Maybe if I know I'll feel better. I'll understand.

His mouth forms a grim line. "I can't tell you that."

"Why? We're part of the same MC now. You know, Angels and Devils and all that mumbo jumbo." Where is my cavalier attitude coming from?

"You need to leave. Now." There is no room for argument in his voice.

"I thought I would come to you, but I can now see that it was a bad idea," I grumble, trying to push him away with my palms on his hard chest.

"I don't see how you thought it would be a good idea. You can't be here right now. Go, Bella. Now."

I get the hell out of there, passing Jeremiah on the way. He calls my name, but I ignore him, all but dive into my car and leave.

I knew coming here was a bad idea, but I guess I just want to be more involved in River's world.

I want it to be our world.

But shit, maybe I don't want to be part of his world at all.

Chapter Six

River

"Fucking hell," I mutter to myself, covering my face with my hands. I shouldn't have yelled at her like that, but when I saw the blood on me, I just panicked. She shouldn't have someone with literal blood on their hands touching her soft, perfect skin.

Just minutes before she walked into the garage, I was getting information out of our hostage. When I saw her, I thought I was dreaming for a moment.

My two worlds don't need to collide, because one is heaven and one is hell.

Fucking hell.

After taking thirty minutes to calm myself down, I find Jeremiah sitting at the dining table. "I saw her run out."

"You shouldn't have let her come down there in the first place," I snap, angry that he let that happen.

"What were you thinking? I should beat the shit out of you."

He puts his hands up. "She was here with me one second and gone the next. I'm sorry. And I wasn't even sure if you were still down there."

Clenching my teeth, I eye the food she brought over for me, the food Jeremiah has clearly helped himself to, which just annoys me further. I wash my hands properly and then serve a plate, sitting at the table alone; Jeremiah's smart enough to hightail it out of here.

I fucked up, and I know I did. I probably scared her, and that's the one thing I never wanted to do. I pull out my phone from my jeans pocket and send her a text.

River: I'm sorry. Can I come see you tonight? And the food is delicious, by the way, thank you.

My eyes are on my phone as I finish the meal, waiting for her to reply. I feel like shit eating the food, knowing she thought of me and brought it here, and I acted like a psychopath. I suppose I wasn't expecting to see her, and I wasn't in the headspace to do so.

I was in the headspace for motherfucking torture and breaking that man to get what I need from him. And being so close, I was focused and very intent on that and that only.

Does she now realize how fucked-up I am?

Maybe she's reconsidering wanting to be with me. I guess I would understand, but it would be hard as fuck to let her go. I don't know if I could. I know she's the woman I want to be with, above all others, and I would never find anyone else that I would feel that way about.

She's irreplaceable.

Priceless.

And I need her to be patient with me.

She finally replies, putting me out of my misery.

Bella: Okay, I'll see you then.

Closing my eyes, I take a deep breath.

The sad truth is I don't think any woman could love the real me.

So Bella is never going to know that side of me.

Ever.

I show up with flowers and what I hope is an apologetic smile.

"I'm sorry," I say as soon as she opens the door. Her eyes go straight to the red tulips. "I wasn't expecting you, and it caught me off guard. And I had some blood on my hand and it just...yeah, I'm sorry. I hope you can forgive me."

She takes my flowers and I step inside, closing the door behind me.

"You had blood on your hand? That's why you freaked out?" she asks, brow furrowing.

"Yes, and my hand was touching your face and... I don't know."

"Don't lie to me."

"What do you mean? I'm not."

"How did you get blood on your hand?"

Shit.

"I can see your mind thinking of a million different answers. Let's skip the bullshit. Just tell me the truth."

I'm quiet for a bit, trying to find the best way out of this. I can't tell her the truth. Can I?

"I'm not lying. There was blood on my hands. That's all."

She stares at me for a long while. For the first time, I cannot see what she sees. She shutters her expression from me, giving me a blank look that I never want to see on her beautiful face again. "That's your one, River."

"My one what?" I ask, trying to reach for her.

She steps back and points a finger at me. "Your one time you can lie to me. You do it again and this is done."

I'm surprised by her tone and don't know how I feel about this.

"That sounds like an ultimatum." I don't like being told what I can or cannot do. Even by Bella.

She shrugs. "It's not. It's a fact. I'm giving you a choice. You can choose to continue to lie to me after this or you can choose to tell me the truth. It's really your choice. I will accept you don't want to tell me the truth about what I saw today. But it's the last time I'll be okay with that. We are a team. We do not keep things from each other. That is what I'm signing up for."

She says it so easily. Like she's not asking me to lay my soul out on display for her. I want to tell her the truth. I want to be a team. But I don't think she'll like what she hears. Can I risk that?

I watch her watching me and I know that she's endgame. I don't want to lose her. I don't know what I would do if I did. And if that means I have to show her who I am, then I will.

"Understood. It won't happen again," I say, and nod.

I follow her as she leads us into her kitchen and starts digging through the cupboard for a vase. "The food was amazing. Romeo came in and ate the remainder of it."

"Good, I'm glad," she replies, filling the glass vase in her hands with water and organizing the flowers in it. "I sent a lot because I knew that some of them would want some."

I love that she thinks of my MC brothers, even my cousin, that asshole Jeremiah.

Once the vase is presentable, she turns to me, and I open my arms out to her. She hesitates for a split second, but then comes to embrace me and presses her cheek against my chest. This woman is my whole heart.

"Have you eaten tonight?" she asks.

I smile against her hair. "You trying to fatten me up?"

She touches my stomach and laughs. "Maybe. It's going to take a lot of cooking."

I lift her up to sit on the countertop and kiss her deeply, catching her off guard. "I did eat, but I'm still a little hungry…"

She wraps her legs around me as I head for her bedroom, our lips still connected. I place her down on the bed, spread her thighs and slide down her silky pajama pants. She's not wearing anything underneath. I tease her a little, kissing up her thighs and focusing everywhere except her sex, until she's squirming in anticipation.

"River," she moans, lifting her hips.

I love the sound of her pleading, so I give her what she wants and lick her pussy, tasting every inch of her. She shudders each time my tongue touches her clit, and I drag out her pleasure as much as I can, until she holds my head down and I give in and make her come. She takes a pillow and places it over her face to muffle her cries, and I keep my mouth on her until she sags back against the bed.

Then I strip down and push the pillow away from her, sliding inside her wet pussy. A growling sound escapes my throat as I look down at her, kissing her lips and slowly moving in and out.

I trace my lips across her jaw and down her neck; I know much she loves to be kissed there and how much it turns her on. She pushes me onto my back and starts to ride me, while looking down at me. She loves this position, where she gets to take control, and I love seeing her like that. She plays with her breasts, squeezing her nipples and putting on a show for me. I reach forward and play with her clit, wanting her to come a second time before I get to finish.

And when she does, it's like a chain reaction, because I come right after, finishing inside her. She lies on top of me afterward, with me still in her, and I slowly feel myself harden again with every movement she makes.

She looks up and smiles at me, and then begins to slide my cock in and out. If it's round two she wants, I'm more than up for it.

I roll her onto her stomach, put a pillow under her hips, then slide in from behind.

We both moan together.

If only we can just live in this bubble. This only perfect piece of my world.

I can never get enough of her, and lucky for me, the feeling is more than mutual.

Chapter Seven

Bella

River stays the night, but I can't sleep. I am sure he thinks we're fine and maybe we are, but something is still not sitting well with me.

I need to figure out if I want to live this life. A life with half-truths and violence. I think I can get over the violence if there was truth. But he can't even give me that. I know I love him. I just don't know if I can forget what I saw. Or forget what he does for the club.

As I'm getting ready for the morning, I open one of Sally's twenty emails that I didn't answer yesterday.

To: Bella Callisto <bella@angelsproperties.com>
From: Sally Henderson <sally@angelsproperties.com>
Subject: URGENT: Lansdale Property—Signature Needed

Bella,
I was able to find the information needed for the Landsdale property, but it needs your signature still. I'm unsure what to do because we need to close by end of day today or else we lose the property and you're not answering your calls. What should I do? Can you please let me know?
Sally

FUCK! I was so preoccupied by what happened with River yesterday that I left the office early and messaged Sally that I wasn't coming back for the day. She sent this email yesterday at 2:30 PM. I've missed the deadline. Julianna is going to be so upset.

I send a text to the seller's real estate agent, playing it cool. Maybe he didn't realize the paperwork was unsigned.

Bella: Hey Tom, everything still good with the Landsdale property?

I cross my fingers and toes. I see the three dots working. Of course he's up this early working.

Tom: Bella! Yes I was messengered the paperwork yesterday right before 5pm. Everything looks good. Drinks to celebrate next week?

Did he miss that the papers weren't signed? I respond to Sally's email.

To: Sally Henderson <sally@angelsproperties.com>
From: Bella Callisto <bella@angelsproperties.com>
Subject: Re: URGENT: Lansdale Property—Signature
Needed

Sally,
I'm so sorry about this. Was this handled? What
happened with this?
Bella

She won't respond until she's in the office. She's
one of those "I stick to working hours only" and I actually admire that about her. And if Tom says everything
is good, then I am not worried. If there is a signature
still missing, I'll correct it today. I make a mental note
to look at the copies as soon as I get into the office.

Instead of worrying, I make River and me some
breakfast and queue some music videos on. When a
certain one comes on, I get distracted and spend the
next four minutes sobbing.

When he comes into the kitchen and sees me crying, he rushes over, worried. "What's wrong, Bella?
Why are you crying? I will kill whoever made you
this upset—"

I cry harder. "No, don't kill him. It's just, I watched
Lewis Capaldi's new music video and now I can't stop
crying."

He pauses, studying me. "What?"

I restart the video clip and hand it to him. "Watch
it and you will understand."

Anything with animals in it makes me cry, I can't help it.

He leans back against the counter and watches it, and then looks over at me, blue eyes as gentle as I've ever seen them. "You are very cute, you know that?"

I'm still wiping my eyes at this point. "How did that not make you cry, how?"

"It was very sad," he admits, pulling me against him and stroking my back. "Anything with animals in it can be hard to watch."

"I know," I whimper, looking over at Hades, safe and warm in his bed. "I need to go and hug my dog right now." He laughs and lets go of me as I all but climb into Hades's bed and love on him. "Never leave me."

He licks my face in return, and I take that as we have a deal.

River finishes up breakfast for us, and we eat it in the garden, sitting on the rattan love seat together. I do love the man. I meant what I said, though. I will not be in a relationship with someone who lies to me. I need to know what I'm getting into or else how can I really know the man I'm in love with? He obviously has some demons, but I know that he would never hurt me. I probably sound like an idiot with those famous last words, but I truly believe them. It's what's keeping me here.

Romeo calls River, sending us back into reality, and he leaves to the clubhouse while I get ready for work. When I get in the office, I pull up the paperwork from the Lansdale deal and see that my signature is in fact on the paperwork. Only I don't remember signing it. Did Sally forge my name?

When Sally comes in, she brings coffee and doughnuts.

"Sally, can you come into my office for a moment?" I say.

She walks in. Sally is a petite woman with girlish features, someone who is hard to be angry at, but I can't let this one slide.

"Close the door," I say, and take a breath. I'm still not quite sure how to play this. Do I berate her and tell her to never do it again? But at the same time, she saved a hundred-million-dollar project. I can't condone this behavior but at the same time I can't yell at her for it. Shit. What would Julianna do?

"What happened with the Lansdale project?" Instead of making assumptions, I want to let her say her piece.

She starts wringing her hands. "Well, I emailed you and then I kept waiting for you to return to the office or call or email back. But it was 4 PM and I knew the papers needed to be in the seller's agent's office by five. So I started calling the emergency numbers you gave me, starting with Julianna."

Okay, she is smart, she did all the right things. And I have to own my fuckup here.

She continues, "But no one was picking up until I got in touch with Rosalind Callisto. I think she's Julianna's sister? She said she'd be right in. You have on the information sheet that any Callisto can sign paperwork, so she signed. But…"

I sigh. "But you saw that she signed *my* name."

Sally nods. "By the time she left, it was 4:45 and I knew if I left I could drive down to the seller's agency to deliver the paperwork. So I made copies and delivered them. I'm so sorry. I didn't know what to do. I assumed since Rosalind was a Callisto that she'd have authority, but I didn't realize. Am I in trouble?"

Sally starts to tear up and I stand to give her a tissue. This is all my fault. My distractions almost cost a big deal. It put this poor girl in an uncomfortable position when all she did was follow directions. And fucking Rosalind. She's been a wild card ever since she found out that Julianna was with Romeo, who she apparently was sleeping with before he met her sister.

"Sally, you did nothing wrong. I'm sorry you're in this position. Please forget about it and I'll figure out the best way to handle this." I usher her out and sit back at my desk going over the possible solutions. I decide to call her.

"Hey, bitch, it's been a while since you called," Rosalind says in a cheerful tone. "What's up? My sister's an old married woman now, so you want to live it up?" Rosalind used to be so fun and easygoing. Over the last year she has turned bitter. I definitely went Team Julianna after everything went down and I haven't been a great cousin.

"Hey, Ros, thanks for helping out at the office

yesterday. Sally says you stopped by to sign some paperwork?"

"Yup, and you're welcome."

I decide to just cut to the chase. "Ros, why did you sign my name? You know you are capable of signing your name on paperwork."

Rosalind laughs. "I was doing it for you. This is the first big deal you're doing without Julianna and I didn't want people to know that you fucked it up."

"I would've dealt with it. You put both me and Sally in a difficult situation. The signature doesn't even match my own."

She grunts, clearly over the conversation. "Please. No one will look at it. Is this what I get for doing you a favor?"

I take a deep breath and realize that what is done is done. "Thank you. Please, next time, just sign your own name."

"Aye aye, Captain," she says, and hangs up on me, clearly annoyed.

I know Rosalind forged my signature. But it was for the greater good. Would anyone ever really find out? Will it make a difference? Making a bigger deal out of this could get us into deeper trouble, so I decide to do nothing.

Including not telling Julianna. I don't want to cause any more stress on her and there is nothing she can do about it now. It's like telling someone you cheated on them after the fact. What good comes from that? People only do that to make themselves feel better. I don't want to know that shit. And yes, I may be in the minority here, but as much as people say "I would want to know," I call bullshit. Let me live in my ignorant bliss.

As soon as I think it, I realize what a hypocrite I am. I just spent the last two days demanding honesty from River. Do I really want to know what he does for the club? Do I want to know what he does to those who threaten the people he loves? Shit, I don't know anymore.

Julianna surprises me on my lunch break, and unlike River, I'm thrilled, despite the secret I'm taking to my grave. We go to this cute little café I've been wanting to try for a while. They sell these thick yet light, fluffy pancakes that make my mouth water just to think about.

"I'm so happy we came here," I say, scanning the menu.

"Me too, I was craving some pancakes," she replies, smiling at me. "What have you been up to?"

"What did you hear?" I ask, arching my brow.

"That you went to the clubhouse yesterday and were seen running out," she says, eyes wide. "What happened? Romeo didn't know the whole story."

I give her a quick rundown. She goes quiet, which means that she knows something but doesn't want to tell me. "Come on, just say it."

"Okay, but don't say anything to River, because he would kill me if he knew I told you. I heard Romeo on the phone and then he told me everything," she says, lowering her voice. "Apparently they found some guy following them and River brought him back to the clubhouse. Like he's still there. That's probably why he freaked out so bad."

My lips open, then close. "I walked in on Romeo using some guy as a punching bag."

Julianna looks at me. She's not surprised.

"You knew."

She nods.

"So you know that this is something River does regularly?"

She reaches for my hand. "Bella, he's the enforcer. What did you think he did?"

When she says it like that, I feel dumb. "I guess I never gave it any thought." And it's true. Ignorance is bliss. But do I want to stay ignorant?

"Does Romeo tell you most things that go on in the club, then?" I ask Julianna, leaning toward her over the table and whispering. "I mean, I know it's different for you—you're leading us with him."

"Yes, I need to know everything going on. But the little details about any violence? Romeo isn't going to give those to me, especially when I'm pregnant. I get the PG version, and that's how I like it," she explains, tucking her blonde hair back behind her ear.

"River tells me nothing, and I know I'm not as involved in the MC as you, but I'm still a part of it," I grumble.

She surprises me by laughing. "You've never cared about what goes on in the MC. You just want to know what River's up to."

"I gave him an ultimatum. Sort of."

Julianna raises her eyebrows, her lips quirking to the side.

"I know, I know. I told him he couldn't lie to me. That this was the one time I'd let him get away with lying to me."

"Brave," she says with both admiration and trepidation in her voice.

"What?" I ask. I can tell she's fighting to not say something.

"Bella, I love you. But you don't want to know the truth. You want to live in your world where there are fairies and princes and you get to live happily ever after."

I am taken aback. She's not wrong, but it makes me sound like a child.

"There is nothing wrong with that. I love that about you. But you shied away from the MC for years—your whole life, really. And now you want to be all up in its business? *I* don't want to know everything and I am in charge of it. Think hard about what you're asking."

My lip twitches, because she's right, and of course she called me out on it. "As if you wouldn't be curious?"

"Oh, I definitely would be. I'm not judging you one bit. River is so mysterious, too. That would do my head in, too," she replies, amusement dancing in her blue eyes. She leans back in her seat and puts her hand on her stomach. "He's definitely an enigma.

Look, I'm not going to sugarcoat it. I've heard that River is a bit of a hothead. He *is* the MC's enforcer. He does it for the Angels too now."

That is new information. I had no idea he was handling the Devils *and* Angels, too.

"Okay, dumb question. What does an enforcer do?" I whisper. I have known he is one. But I never stopped to ask what that means exactly.

Julianna leans in. "He enforces," she whispers before breaking out into laughter.

I can't help the giggles that come out. "Julianna," I whine.

"Okay, okay. Real talk. He's the muscle. When they need someone to get someone to talk, River comes in. When they need someone to be in charge of cleaning up…after certain things, they call River."

I knew all this. But hearing it and picturing it, I don't know how I feel.

"Does he like…kill people?" I ask, knowing the answer but needing confirmation.

All the laughter is gone from Julianna's face. "What I will tell you is what I know for sure. Even after what happened to me, Romeo allowed River to handle Victor."

I look at her with questions in my eyes. What does that mean? "But—"

"That is all I will ever say about Victor, Bella. I'm done talking about this."

And there is the president of the Angels. She looks down at her menu again and I process what she said.

Victor, who Julianna originally was betrothed to, got into a fight with Matthew, who was River's brother, and Matthew died. Victor also beat up Julianna. Victor is also no longer with us, and the club is better for it. But I didn't realize that River was the person responsible for his death. I can't turn a blind eye to this, and while the sight is uglier than I have ever believed, I still can't convince myself to walk away. How many people has he killed? Do I even want to know? How much of this truth can I handle?

Julianna looks up and must see my brain working a mile a minute. "I've never seen him softer than when he is around you," she says to comfort to me.

"Does it bother you?" I ask. "Knowing what they did. What they are capable of."

She shakes her head. "No. It wasn't done in haste. Sometimes people do bad shit for good reasons. And I believe that given the chance I would've done the same thing."

"I don't know how to feel about that."

"That's okay. You don't need to decide now. But you will need to decide eventually. And I'll love you no matter what you land on."

I appreciate that, and right now I don't know how I feel. I do know I don't want to live without him. Does that make me a bad person?

My mind is a total mess right now.

I force a smile and decide I need to lighten the mood up. "Corey told me I must be really good in bed," I state, and Julianna makes a sound of laughter mixed with choking.

"Is that what she said? What, to have kept River's attention that long?" she asks, on the verge of laughter again.

"To be known as his girlfriend, I'm guessing," I mutter, shaking my head. I want to mention the cuts I saw on her wrists, but I figure that's not really my business. I don't want her to hate me after only meeting her once. But I also don't want her to get hurt and I didn't say anything, so I feel very torn.

"Like that's all you have to offer?" Julianna replies with a roll of her eyes. "It's nice to see Corey being more of herself these days. She took the loss of her brother Matthew so hard. And it still hurts to know the Angels MC was behind that. What a senseless loss of life."

"I know, I can't imagine how hard it must be for her," I say, really feeling for her. I'm an only child, but I love Julianna like my sister, and I'd be devastated if anything happened to her. "River loves her so much and tries to be there for her in his own way."

"He does," she agrees, nodding. "Corey told me he'd always protect her and his mother. He was their hero. I think Matthew was the one who was more there for her emotionally, though."

"Yeah, I can't imagine River being too emotionally open," I admit, experiencing that firsthand.

Our soufflé pancakes arrive, and they are as perfect as I imagined. I can't help but be one of those people and take a photo of the meal before I taste it.

Julianna softly moans. "Wow, this is so good. We are coming back here. The baby approves."

"Yes, we are," I agree.

Sometimes a lunch date with your cousin is all the therapy you need.

Chapter Eight

River

"You bringing Bella to the party?" Corey asks. She's sitting on the countertop in the clubhouse kitchen, eating toast and drinking coffee.

"What party?" I ask, yawning. I didn't sleep as well last night without Bella in bed next to me, and I plan on rectifying that tonight.

"Jeremiah's birthday."

Ah, shit. I'd forgotten all about that. "I'll see if she's free," I comment, pouring myself some coffee.

"Cool. Especially now that there's no man hidden in the garage," Corey says, in a chirpy tone that doesn't match her words one bit.

My lips tighten. I guess everyone has fucking heard about that, then. "Don't you have somewhere to be?"

"Nope, no classes today," she replies, dusting crumbs off her fingers. "And I'm helping Julianna get everything ready for tomorrow. You guys eat a lot of food, you know that? And don't get me started on the amount of alcohol we are going to need. Even though there have been a few parties, I still can't get used to the Angels coming around. Will be interesting to see how that goes down." She jumps off and lands easily on her feet, and leaves without another word.

I send Bella a text before I forget, because I would love to have her here for the party. Corey is right—without our captive here, I can now relax. It turned out that he was a hired hit man coming after Romeo. He didn't know who put the hit out. All he knew was that it was a woman, and she was paying him fifty thousand dollars. Unfortunately, Roger is not going to get a chance to use that fifty thousand. Unless being buried in the middle of the desert counts.

As sad as it is, our first thought is that it's our grandmother Cathy.

And ain't that a hard pill to swallow.

Cathy was basically kicked out of the family for her betrayal and alliance with Victor, who also ended up being her grandson. She went against all of us, planning to have Victor take over the Devils and Angels, and we thought she was in our past. But now we have to wonder if she's capable of wanting Romeo dead.

There is a small part of me that wants to believe that it's not her at all. She's my blood and the woman I ran to when my father was too much when I was a kid. She used to be a comfort to me and I have to think that there is still some good in her.

River: There's a party here tomorrow night for Jeremiah's birthday. You in?

Bella: Yes, I'd love to. I'll pick up a gift for him.

River: It's okay, don't worry about it.

Bella: Can't show up empty-handed.

She's so fucking cute.

River: Don't waste your money on him.

Knowing her, she'll bring something anyway, but I don't want her to feel like she has to. Corey is right, though, this will be the first party with our MCs united. Although we are now one MC, they've stuck to their clubhouse and we've stuck to ours—it's what we know, and we've all been comfortable with that. But of course everyone has been invited tonight, and although it might be awkward, I think the more events we do like this the more comfortable everyone will get with each other. At the end of the day, we want the same thing, and we care about the same people. And that's all it comes down to. We will all be able to thrive, financially and in power, and what more could an MC want?

We are now untouchable.

Except from my grandmother, apparently.

Maybe.

Shit.

* * *

After staying the night at Bella's, I leave early morning, get in a workout in our gym, shower and then get ready to be bossed around by Julianna to make sure the clubhouse is ready for the influx of people. I'm not the most social person in the world, but even I'm looking forward to tonight, and seeing the whole family together.

I invited my mom, but she doesn't want to come. I'd say the reason she doesn't come here anymore is because we lost Matthew, but really that's not true. She turned her back on MC life a long time ago, right when she lost the sight in her eye, and when my father went missing. Her life changed when she walked away from him, and I think for her that meant leaving the MC behind, too. I don't blame her at all either.

Once upon a time it was a different story. Mom was very involved with her family, and helped raise Romeo when her sister, Romeo's mother, Victoria, wasn't doing too much of a good job of it. But no one had my mother's back when my father started beating on her, because he was the son of an MC president, and she was just a woman. I guess everyone has their limits, even people you see as the strongest.

Especially those people.

When the sun starts to set people start arriving. Corey does help out a lot, and I appreciate seeing that sparkle back in her eyes, even if bossing people around is what brings that back. Losing Matthew hit us all, but it hurt her the most. Matthew was the best brother. He was kind, patient and emotionally intelligent. I can protect her, and be there for her, but I will never be what Matthew was.

It should have been me that died. We all know it, and the guilt that I'm burying beneath my feet still tries to trip me over whenever it can.

I try not to think about it, and him, and although that's not the best coping mechanism, it's the only one I have right now.

I wait out front until Bella arrives in her BMW, and open the door for her. She pulls out a present wrapped in fancy black paper and a gold bow and gets out of the car with a red-lipped smile.

"You look beautiful," I comment, taking in her black dress and heels. She smells like heaven, her perfume fruity and sweet, and I don't know how the fuck she's mine, but I'm glad that she is. "I knew you'd get him a present anyway." I smirk, taking her hand and leading her inside.

"It's rude to show up somewhere empty-handed," she reminds me, smiling at Romeo and Julianna, who approach us first.

Julianna hugs her and drags her away from me before I can say anything. I see her wish Jeremiah a happy birthday and give him the gift from the living room.

"Did you locate her?" Romeo asks, while keeping his eyes on his wife.

"Not yet."

He sighs. "Well, tonight is for fun, so let's not worry about all of that until tomorrow."

My eyes narrow as I see Jeremiah hugging Bella, and lingering a little too long. "Someone wants to die on their birthday."

Romeo follows my line of sight and laughs, slapping me on the shoulder. "Never thought I'd see you fall in love. Please, don't start any fights. Wow, did his hand just touch her ass?" I growl and he pulls me back. "Shit, I'm just joking. Calm down."

Leaving him behind, I pull Bella away from my cousin. "Do you want something to drink?"

"Sure," she replies, smiling up at me. "Why do you look so angry? It's a party!" She does a little dance and winks.

She's so damn cute.

I get a beer, while Bella opts for a red wine. We head outside in the backyard, the music getting louder with each step. I see Corey sitting on one of the big speakers, drink in hand, a hot dog in the other. I'm about to go over to her when a man approaches her. The two of them speak, and she laughs.

Damon.

He's one of the Angels and Julianna's friend, and I don't know how he knows my sister or how well, but I'm going to go and find out.

Bella pulls me back, brow furrowing. "Let her have some fun. She's an adult."

"Barely."

"We're right here, we can see what they are up to.

Everyone can," she says with a shrug, pulling me to the dance floor. "Come on, dance with me."

Pressing her body against mine, she wraps her arms around me and rotates her hips seductively. If she wants to distract me, it's working.

She smiles, and I follow suit.

Fuck.

I guess it is a party, right?

Chapter Nine

Bella

While almost everyone else keeps their cups flowing, I stop after two, not wanting to get too drunk. I notice River only has one beer and that's it. In fact, I've never seen him drunk—the man is always in control. He has been nothing but attentive all night, introducing me to people I haven't met, and making sure I'm okay. Julianna comes and sits with me, looking out on the dance floor, while River and Romeo chat with Echo, the manager at their burlesque nightclub. I've never been there, but Echo is a very attractive woman, and River seems to be close with her.

"I had lunch with Rosalind today," she's saying, but I can't look away from the woman standing a little too closely to my man.

"How was that?" I ask her. I still don't trust Rosalind, and I don't think I ever will. But I understand she is Julianna's sister, and I know she's making an effort to work on their relationship.

"Fine. I think she's trying, you know? And they're all just work colleagues and friends, trust me," Julianna says, reading my mind. "She's a cool chick. Kind of standoffish, but when you get to know her, she's really nice."

"Good to know," I reply, forcing myself to look away from them. I trust River, and I'm usually not a jealous person at all, but with him I can't seem to help myself. Not that I'd ever let him know that. I don't remember feeling jealous even once with Mark. Maybe because deep down I didn't care and knew that he liked me more than I did him. Or maybe it's because I know that bikers are never short of female attention.

And River? He's a ten out of ten.

Brutally handsome, badass and a secret sweet side that only I can apparently see.

I wouldn't let go of that without a fight.

"Romeo's parents are here," she says, sounding surprised. "I didn't think they were coming."

"How's your relationship with them going?" Romeo and Julianna getting together was a big shock to everyone, and I know both families are still getting used to the fact.

"A little better now that I'm pregnant," she admits, resting her palm on her stomach. Her giant diamond sparkles on her finger. "But it's not great. I don't know if it ever will be. But we are all polite and civil, so that's what matters."

His mom, Victoria, downs her glass of alcohol. Julianna looks over at me and shrugs. "She can be a little problematic sometimes, I'm not going to lie. It sounds like River's mom, Lisa, raised Romeo more than Victoria did."

"Have you met Lisa?" I ask, curious. River rarely talks about his family, and when he does it's usually about Corey. He doesn't mention Matthew, his mother or father. And I don't push, I figure he will talk about them when he's good and ready.

"No, I haven't. I've only seen photos of her. She's kind of kept to herself since Matthew died. Romeo said River bought her a house. And her and Corey have a strained relationship, too," she says, so only I can hear. "I know River goes and sees her. I think they are quite close."

"He doesn't talk about her much," I admit, wondering why that is. "He hasn't taken me to meet her yet either. Should that be something I should be concerned about?" Maybe he thinks she won't like me, or maybe she's one of those mothers who doesn't like any woman her son ends up with. What do they call them? Boy moms?

"Really? Romeo reminisces about their childhood, and Aunty Lisa is usually in the stories. She had a big impact on him. He calls her up now and again, and he's been out to see her a few times."

"What about River's dad?" I ask, realizing he hasn't been mentioned once.

Julianna goes quiet for a moment before answering. "I haven't heard much about him, but what I have heard isn't good. But I think you need to ask River about it yourself."

Which is code for she doesn't want to get in trouble for giving me too much information. Frustrating, but she's right. It should come from River himself and no one else.

"That's fair enough. Wow, your mother-in-law is now downing tequila shots," I say, grinning.

"She must not get out often," Julianna replies in a dry tone. "And is it just me, or is Damon hitting on Corey? Wow, he has some balls on him. No one ever dares to talk to Corey in case it pisses River off."

"Yeah, River did see him. I had to distract him so he didn't go over there and cause a scene. Should I warn Damon?" I ask, not wanting to give the men something to fight over. We don't need any extra drama happening, please and thank you.

"If you tell him to leave her alone, he'll just want her more. You know what men are like. They like the forbidden."

"You'd know," I tease, and she laughs out loud.

"Yes, I do. That's why there's no point saying anything. Who knows, maybe she won't like him."

We share a look and giggle. Damon is fucking hot, there's no other way to put it. He's got gray eyes that see into your soul, a head full of dark hair and a smile that could charm his way in and out of anything.

I just need to hope that "anything" isn't River's baby sister, who already has enough going on right now.

River comes over to check on me, standing behind my chair. He pushes my hair to the side and kisses my neck from behind. "Can I get you anything?"

"I'm okay, thank you."

He looks to Julianna. "And you, Miss Preggers? You want juice or something? Romeo to give you a foot rub?"

"Actually, could you get me a jar of pickles from the fridge and a straw?" she asks, flashing a hopeful glance his way.

River nods, keeping a straight face, until Romeo appears. "Your wife wants some pickles and a straw."

Romeo smirks, looking down at her. "More pickles?"

"Is yours not good enough?" River jokes, laughing under his breath at his own joke.

Romeo goes after him, the two play-fighting.

"I'll never get my pickles," Julianna sighs, so I get up and head into the kitchen to go and retrieve them for her. When a pregnant woman wants something, you make sure she has it.

"And who do we have here?" asks a smooth, deep voice belonging to a man about my age, wearing jeans and a white T-shirt with a navy cap. He slides over to me with nothing but confidence in his green eyes and, as the young people call it now, rizz. "You are fucking gorgeous. Where have you been all my life?" He moves to put his arm around me.

Jeremiah lifts his head out from behind the fridge

door and laughs. I didn't even notice him there. "She's River's."

The man drops his hand and moves to the other side of the room faster than Usain Bolt. "I'm so sorry, I had no idea," he explains, wincing, while a drunk Jeremiah just laughs at him again. He turns his cap backward, and it looks even better on him that way.

"That's Jag. Ignore him—he's a prospect," Jeremiah says, still rooting around in the fridge, pulling out more alcohol.

"Nice to meet you, Jag," I reply, grinning, while he leans back on the counter, looking like he's going to be sick. I turn back to Jeremiah. "Can you pass me the pickle jar, please?"

He arches a brow, but reaches in and hands me the giant jar. I grab a straw off the table and head back out.

"You're not going to tell him, are you?" Jag calls out, sounding both hopeful and terrified. I shake my head, and he sighs in relief.

As I walk back over to Julianna, everything is starting to fall into place. After seeing him in the garage, I now understand why everyone is so scared of the man I love.

Chapter Ten

River

While Bella and Julianna disappear into the bath-room together, Romeo's mother, Aunty Victoria, finds me alone in the kitchen and comes for a chat.

"How's my sister?" she asks, taking a sip of her drink. She's gone hard on the spirits tonight, and I wonder if there's a reason for it, or if she's just in the mood to party.

"She's good," I reply, pulling a chair out and sit-ting down. "She's happy. You should give her a call sometime."

"I tried," she admits, shrugging. "She doesn't want to have much to do with me, it seems. We used to be close. We were more than just sisters—we were best friends when we met your father and my husband. I pretty much took care of her for her entire life."

That is not the version of the story that I heard. "Really? I thought she was more the caregiver."

Aunty Victoria laughs and takes another drink. Her hair is messy, her makeup smeared and it looks like she's had a rough night. "Maybe, maybe. But she owes me. She knows why. You know we never talk about Robert anymore. But he's not Voldemort—why can't we talk about him? He did exist, you know."

"Oh, trust me. I know," I mutter.

The bastard haunts me and he always will. He was an abusive man, with a bad temper and a drinking problem, and he made our lives hell.

Until one day I fought back and sent him to his own hell. Now we are all living our best lives without him.

Victoria grabs the chair next to me and sits down, her drink spilling in the process. "She always worried about you, you know. With everything that happened. You took it all on. You shielded Matthew and Corey, and you protected her as best as you could."

"I don't think—"

She laughs without humor, cutting me off. "But even with all that she didn't tell you the truth. The reason why Robert hated you so much."

This is rich. "What, I didn't like being a punching bag?"

"Robert wasn't even your biological dad. He hated you because you reminded him of your mother's infidelity."

My blood turns to ice.

What the fuck?

"What do you mean?" I demand, leaning forward

and looking her in the eye. "Robert wasn't my father?"

"I don't know how they all kept it under wraps for so long."

What she says next, in her drunken stupor, stops me in my tracks.

"Andrew is your father. That's right. My husband fucked his own brother's wife. Why do you think I let her raise Romeo with you? Might as well keep the brothers together, right? And after all these years I think it's time the truth came out."

Romeo is my half brother?

This can't be true.

Maybe she's just drunk and making something up.

Or maybe the truth is finally coming out after all of these years.

I don't know.

While she keeps on ranting about how my mother betrayed her, my life flashes before my eyes. I thought I knew who I was. The son of an angry man who could never control his temper. A temper I inherited, or so I thought.

I guess that answers the question, then.

Environment wins over genetics.

Bella steps into the kitchen, resting her hand on the doorframe, smiling widely. Her lipstick is still perfectly put on, unlike the woman next to me. "There you are. Julianna is calling it a night."

"Do you want to go home?" I ask, standing and feeling relieved to have a way out of this conversation.

"She's a beautiful girl," my aunt comments, looking between the two of us. She too stands up, wobbling, and grabs a bottle of wine with her on her way out, with no idea or care of the damage her words have just inflicted.

"Yeah, I think I'm ready to go," Bella says, pulling me from my thoughts. She takes my hand in her much smaller one. "But you can stay and keep on partying—I can get myself home."

"If you think I'd let you go home alone in the middle of the night, you must be crazy," I comment, leaning down to kiss her. "Let me make sure Romeo doesn't need me for anything."

We find him outside, watching Jeremiah doing a shoey. For those that don't know, that's when you pour alcohol into a shoe and drink from it like a glass.

"Classy," Corey calls out, shaking her head. Damon isn't with her, and for that I'm thankful. Last thing my sister needs right now is a man. She needs to focus on college, not some pretty boy. Let alone an Angel pretty boy.

"I'm going to take Bella home," I say to Romeo, who nods. "You all good if I bail?"

"Yeah, go ahead," he replies, slapping me on the back. "I'm going myself. Julianna has had enough."

"Most of us have." Aunty Victoria's words echo in my ear, and I try to drown them out. Now is not the time to address this. I need to be alone with my girl. I can deal with the rest later.

"Not the birthday boy," Romeo laughs.

I notice Jag, our new recruit, looking at me, and I arch my brow at him. He pales. No idea what that is about, but right now I just want to get my woman home and be naked in bed with her.

We all say our goodbyes, and I drive us in Bella's car back to her house, where I strip her down and taste every inch of her. It's the best kind of distraction. After she's come twice, she gets down on her knees and takes as much of my cock as she can into her sweet mouth.

I don't last long, but I make up for it when I fuck her slowly afterward, torturing and teasing her, making her come over and over again.

The next morning Bella can tell something is off with me, but I'm not ready to talk to her or anyone about what Aunty Victoria told me until I find out the truth. After having breakfast with Bella, I drive straight to my mom's house to get some answers.

"River, what are you doing here?" she asks as she opens the door. She must notice the expression on my face. "Is everything okay?" She steps back to let me inside.

"I need to ask you a question," I say, pacing up and down her living room, while she takes a seat on the brown leather couch.

"What is it?" she asks, brow furrowing. She's wearing the cashmere sweater I bought her for Christmas last year, and she crosses her arms over it.

"Is Robert my father?" I ask her, stopping to look her in the eyes. "My biological father."

Her visible eye widens, the other hidden by the patch, and her face pales. "River—"

"I just want the truth, Mom," I demand, jaw clenching. I need it like I need fucking air.

She looks down at her hands. "No, he's not. Who told you? Victoria?"

I nod. "Yes, she got drunk last night and let it slip. She said Andrew was my father."

My mom starts to cry, covering her face with her hands. "I'm so sorry, River. I know I should have told you, but I didn't want to… I don't know, ruin their family, I guess. We only slept together twice, and it was a mistake. It never should have happened."

"Twice? Once is a mistake. Twice is a plan."

"I know," she sobs.

"Did Robert know?" I ask, swallowing hard.

"Yes, he did," she admits, blinking quickly, her lips pouting in misery. "He knew. We never spoke about it, but inside he knew. The timing of your birth gave it all away."

"But you're sisters…" I say. How could they want to sleep with the same man? Where is the family loyalty?

Mom shrugs, a flash of sadness in her eyes before she shields it. "And they were brothers. But he definitely knew. You know, we met Andrew and your father at the same time. Andrew and I got along well, but your aunt had her eyes set on him and I…stepped aside."

I shake my head in disbelief. Aunty Victoria is a

piece of work, but I can't wrap my head around that Mom kept this from me. "You let me believe that monster was my father! For what? I've spent my whole life trying not to be like him, then blaming him for the way that I am, and he's not even my biological dad?"

She sobs. "He was Matthew and Corey's father—I didn't want you to feel different in any way. Did you think Andrew would want to raise you with Victoria? She barely raised Romeo. He was here, with us."

I continue to pace. "I don't even know what to do with this information."

Romeo is still older than me, which puts me next in line, and if anything were to happen to Romeo, touch wood, the club would go to me. At least until he has a child. While even as Robert's son this would always be the case, being Andrew's son does change the dynamics a little. If I wanted to, I could always fight for my place as the next president. But I don't want that.

I never have.

"Me and Victoria decided it was best that I told Andrew you weren't his," she adds, wincing. More deceit, what a surprise. "He may have his suspicions, but he doesn't know for sure."

"And how do you know for sure?" I ask her, frowning.

"I was pregnant with you before Robert and I were… intimate," she admits, sighing deeply. "Six weeks pregnant. What are you going to do now?"

"I don't know," I say, sitting down. I need time

to process this, because it changes so much for me. Robert has been haunting me this whole time, and he's not even the man who created me.

"How's Corey?" she asks, changing the subject. "Is she doing okay?"

My jaw tenses at the fact that she's so easily done talking about something that changes everything for me. "She's fine. You should call her, or see her," I suggest offhandedly, leaning back on the couch and staring straight ahead at the turned-off television.

The two of them haven't had much of a relationship since Matthew died. Mom needed someone to blame, and instead of me, she took it out on Corey. I suppose their relationship was strained even before that, but losing the glue of the family is what finally broke them. "And is that all you have to say about this?"

"I did the best I could, River," she says after a moment of silence. "I know I messed up, and I never should have slept with Andrew in the first place. The first time it happened was before he and Victoria started seeing one another. Then they had a drunken night together and she got pregnant with Romeo. The second, and last time, we were together it was supposed to be closure. A goodbye. I was going to leave the MC life altogether. But I got pregnant with you, and then Robert showed his interest in me. I should have chosen a man better than Robert to raise you all. I'm so sorry. I took the coward's way out."

I lean over and hug her. There's no point blaming her for anything—she did do her best, and she always loved us. Robert was a piece of shit who took advantage of a nice woman like my mother, and our lives are all better now that he's gone.

"It's okay," I lie, not wanting her to be upset. "I wish you told me the truth, instead of hearing it from Aunty Victoria."

"We both said we'd never speak of it," she says, touching my face with her hand. "It did no one any good to know the truth."

Probably not, but I deserve to know my truth. This has caused a complete identity crisis in me.

I leave her house feeling more confused than ever. But until I process my emotions, I'm going to keep this information to myself.

Chapter Eleven

Bella

Damon appears against the doorframe to my office. I do a double take when I see him, and remove my headphones, which are blasting Ed Sheeran's latest album. "What did you say?"

"I asked what you know about Corey."

I turn back to my laptop. "Hello to you too, Damon. Yes, I am well, thank you. What are you even doing here?"

It's been a couple of nights since the party, so I'm surprised he's obviously still thinking about that. I haven't known Damon to overtly chase women. He kind of stays quiet, and I never really know what he does in his own time. Maybe he *is* a player? I have no idea. But I do know that he's nice, friendly and has a trustworthy vibe about him. I've always liked him, and I know that Julianna feels the same, especially when he showed her loyalty when no one else would.

"Julianna wanted me to drop off some documents," he explains, stepping inside and sitting down on my desk like he owns it. "She's beautiful, don't you think? That red hair. That body. Those hazel eyes."

"Who?" I ask.

"Corey," he says, frowning at my lack of focus. "Pay attention, Bella."

I pause my typing and swivel on my chair to face him. "Yes, she is beautiful. And pretty young don't you think? How about Echo? She has pretty red hair, too." If that's what he is going for. And yes, I know why I'm suggesting Echo.

He nods, running a hand through his hair. "Choices, choices. And how old is Corey, then?"

"I don't know, but young. Twenty, maybe? She only just started college."

"What else do you know about her?" he presses, gray eyes pinned on me waiting for my reply.

Just that he should leave her alone if he knows what's good for him. Don't get me wrong, Damon is badass in his own right.

But River?

I'm discovering that River is a whole different beast.

I roll my eyes. "I'm not your personal matchmaker, Damon. I saw you two talking—why didn't you ask her these things yourself?"

"She's not an open-book type of person," he replies, sounding both disgruntled and amused. He has the sleeves of his black shirt folded up to his forearms, exposing a fancy-looking black watch. "She wasn't too keen on answering any of my questions."

My lip twitches. "Smart girl."

"What do you mean? You don't think I'm a catch?" he asks, placing his hand over his heart in mock sympathy. "I had Julianna's back when shit went down. Don't I get points for that?"

I purse my lips and decide to go with the truth. "You know she's River's sister, right?"

He stills.

Ha.

No, he did not.

"Fuck," he mutters, but doesn't look intimidated, just speculative. "Yeah, I suppose that makes things a little harder. But I can take him."

I snort. "Are you being serious or just delusional?"

Damon laughs. "River is a scary dude. I get it. But he can't control who his sister dates."

"Unless it's you. He's her only living sibling after their brother, Matthew, died," I add, arching my brow. "At the hands of Victor, from our club. And she's the only girl in the family."

He winces, crossing his arms over his chest. "Okay, I hear you. But just because she's River's sister doesn't mean she's going to be single forever. He's going to have to deal with her dating at some point."

"Yes, but it also doesn't mean it has to be you to take her off the market. We don't need any extra drama for Julianna and Romeo," I state, staring him down. "There are plenty of other women out there."

"Wow, calm down. I am taking no one off the market," he says, brow furrowing. "But I'm not going to lie, she did catch my attention. She's not that much younger than me, only a couple of years. What if I ask River first if I can take her out on a date?"

"Well, if I were you, I'd make sure I was serious about her before you did that. Otherwise, I think it can go badly for you. Do you really like her? Or do you just think she's hot and are bored?"

"I've only met her once, I don't know what I think. But I do know that she is intriguing and smart, and attractive," he says, shrugging.

"You could ask, Damon," I agree. "Or you could leave her alone."

And I'd go with the latter.

He leans forward and touches my shoulder. "Thanks for the chat."

"Anytime. I hope you listen to what I've said."

"Yeah, she's off-limits, blah blah blah…" He places a folder on my desk before leaving.

My mother calls me on my lunch break, and I chat with her for a bit. Julianna's mother and mine are sisters, but they couldn't be more different. I think responsibility does that. My mom, Vivian, is a free spirit, and she and my father, Trevor, do a lot of traveling. They are currently at a ski resort, living their lives. With them I was and always will be the third wheel. There's a reason they only had one child; I think they realized that extra responsibility wasn't for them. My dad didn't mind taking the Callisto name either. He fit in well with Paulie, Julianna's dad, and liked being part of the MC. But he really just adored my mother and pretty much would do anything to be with her.

They haven't met River yet. I guess they would have at the party if they'd been here. Is it weird that we still haven't met each other's parents after all this time? Our relationship started out as a secret and was for some time, so I think that's why the introductions have yet to take place.

My phone buzzes with a text.

River: Can you stay here tonight? I miss you.

I smile. He usually stays at mine because it's more private than being at the clubhouse, but I don't mind staying there. It'll give me an opportunity to know his MC brothers and family.

Bella: Sure. What time?

River: Six? I'll come pick you up and take you out for dinner.

Bella: Date night? I'm in.

Being with River is so different from being with Mark, and in a good way. River will always take control and pick me up, organize a date, and he'll always pay. I don't have to worry about anything when I'm with him;

I can just relax and enjoy with no stress in the world. With Mark, we'd usually go halves on the bill, or take turns paying. Not that I don't mind paying, but I know River would be offended if I tried to. I should do it tonight and see his reaction.

I'm smiling as I get home and jump in the shower. I love going out to eat. It's my favorite thing in the world, and the reason I will never be rich—I'd spend the last bit of money I have on food. I don't care if there's food at home.

An hour and one cute black dress later and I'm ready to go. I slide my black leather Alexander McQueen bracelet with the gold skull onto my wrist and spray a splash of perfume on my neck just as River knocks on the door.

"You look so fucking beautiful" is the first thing he says to me.

"Thank you. You look very handsome yourself," I reply, offering him my hand, stepping outside and locking the door behind me. "How was your day?"

"Busy," he replies, stopping in front of his motorcycle and looking down at my bare legs and heels. "Guess we are leaving this behind, then."

I grin and hand him my car keys. I'm more than happy to be a passenger princess when I get the chance.

"How was your day?" he asks once we're buckled in.

"Good, I actually got tons of work done. I would have gotten more if Damon didn't drop in for a chat, but—"

"Damon?" he asks, frowning. "What did he want to chat about?"

Ah, your sister?

"Nothing much. He was just running errands for Julianna," I say, looking out the window. Yeah, I'm not getting in the middle of that one.

"Hmm," he comments.

"What?" I ask, lip twitching. "You don't like Damon?"

He gives me a quick glance before returning his eyes to the road. "He's a good-looking bastard—why the hell would I want him around my woman?"

I laugh. "He doesn't like me. We're just friends. I've known him for years."

"Men and woman are never just friends," he grumbles.

"Oh really?" I fire back, a little too quickly. "Then how about you and Echo?"

"What?" he asks, as his brow furrows. "What about her?"

"You just said men and women can't be friends. And Julianna was telling me how you are all just friends, so which one is it?"

He goes quiet, and I arch my brow waiting for his response. "Well?"

"She works for us—it's a business relationship," he replies, shrugging. "Trust me, you have nothing to worry about. I don't see anyone other than you, Bella. I don't want anyone else. I have fucking tunnel vision when it comes to you."

"And I feel the same way about you," I reply, lifting my chin.

With a panty-dropping smile, he reaches over and touches my thigh.

And I fall in love all over again.

Chapter Twelve

River

After a beautiful seafood dinner, we take a walk and then head back to the clubhouse. Things have been quiet here, a little too quiet, and we can't help but continuously look over our shoulders. Cathy is still gone, and we don't know if she's planning something or is just living her elderly life somewhere.

I wonder if she knows the truth about Andrew.

She seems to have known everything.

I know I should speak to Romeo about finding out the truth of my father. I just don't want things to change, and I know the second it all comes out, it will. I guess I'm just pushing it to the side until I'm ready to deal with it. I can't lie that it's not weighing heavily on me, and I just don't know how to react to learning this information.

"Where is everyone?" Bella asks as we step inside a seemingly empty clubhouse.

"They went out for a ride," I explain, taking her hand and leading her inside. "Do you want anything from the kitchen?"

She touches her stomach. "No, thank you."

I pull her against me and pin her to the wall for a kiss before we hear the rumbling of the motorcycles, and it's not long before the men are piling back inside. Romeo steps in first, surrounded by a whole lot of leather cuts and boots.

"Are we interrupting?" he asks with a smirk. He turns to Bella and winks. "I'm just going to go and pick Julianna up from her parents' house. She'll be happy that you're here. She's been wanting to get you to try some pickle thing you told her about. Apparently it's her favorite thing ever."

Bella laughs, and I could watch her do it all day. Her gray eyes light up and fill with so much fucking joy that I feel happy. "I thought she would like it," she replies, turning to Jeremiah with a smile. "And how are you?"

"Good," he replies, looking to me, then back to her. "Thank you for that bottle of scotch you got me for my birthday—it was delicious."

"You drank it all already?" she asks, amusement in her tone.

"Nope, but it's about halfway through. I had a little help," he replies, looking over at Jag, who shrugs.

"It was good, can confirm," the prospect adds. "Want to try some?"

Bella surprises me by replying with a "Sure" and

then heading to the bar with the men without even checking to see if I'm even following.

They like her, and she likes them, and although a little bit of me wants to keep her to myself, it's important that she feels comfortable here, and that the men care for her. Because if anything ever happened to me, I'd trust them to look out for her and take care of her.

Jeremiah pours her a glass on the rocks as she takes a seat. "For you, my lady." He then pours me and Jag one. "And for the gentlemen."

Bella lifts her glass up for a cheers before taking a sip. "To the Devils and Angels MC."

We all clink.

"Yeah, okay this is pretty good," she admits, licking her lips. "It's strong." She turns to me and adds, "Yeah, yum. I have good taste."

I reach out and touch the back of her neck. If she keeps being so fucking cute, this socializing is going to end real fast, because I'm going to be dragging her back to my bed where I'm going to keep her for the rest of the night.

About an hour later Julianna appears, hugging Bella from behind. "Nice to see you, cousin."

"You, too," Bella replies, smiling widely. "River and I had the best dinner—you have to go there and try the food."

Julianna turns to me. "Since when does River know all the good spots?"

"Since I have a woman who loves to eat," I reply, gently squeezing Bella's nape before letting go.

Hot, Julianna mouths to her.

Romeo spots her and comes over, holding a bag full of…pickles?

"Wow, you weren't kidding," Bella comments, putting her empty glass down and laughing. "I can't believe you went and bought all of that."

Julianna takes the bag from Romeo and gives us a play-by-play on how best to eat them, and Romeo and I look at each other in amusement.

And that's the thing about love.

He'd let her talk about pickles all fucking day without making one penis joke.

While Bella, Jag and Jeremiah get dragged into trying Julianna's creation, Romeo and I find ourselves in the kitchen alone.

"Still no word of Grandma Cathy," he says, stretching his neck from side to side. "She's probably right under our noses watching Grandpa Johnny with his new girlfriend, Libby, waiting to get her revenge."

"It wouldn't surprise me," I admit, opening the fridge and getting out two bottles of water. I know Bella likes to sleep with one next to her in case she wakes up thirsty. "I don't think we should underestimate her. I thought I saw someone following me after leaving Bella's house tonight, but I lost them. Silver car. I don't know if I was being paranoid or not, but I'm going to keep an eye out."

"Yeah, we don't know if there's another hit out for us." Romeo nods, taking a swig of his beer and closing his eyes for a few seconds. "And with Julianna being pregnant, my blood pressure is fucking high, I need to make sure she's safe at all times."

"She will be," I promise him. "Any of us would do anything to keep her and the baby safe, you know that."

"I do. And I don't care how stressed I get as long as she doesn't need to be. I just want her to have a happy and worry-free pregnancy."

"She is," I say, lip twitching. "She wouldn't be going on about fucking pickles with candy and sauce on them if she wasn't having an enjoyable pregnancy. She knows that you have it covered, no matter what."

He smiles. "Good. I read that whatever she feels, the baby does. So I don't want her to be sad or angry or worried. She just needs to be happy and in her bubble, and I'll do the rest."

"The baby will be the happiest baby ever," I say, slapping him on the shoulder.

"This is some good shit," I hear Jag proclaim loudly, followed by the women's laughter. It's been many years since we've taken in new prospects, since we usually keep it in the family, but Romeo thought it might be good to add in some fresh meat, and apparently Jag is someone we want on our side. Not only is he a hacker, he's also ex Special Forces. Although looking at him, you'd never be able to tell. He's always happy, and not someone I would peg as being extremely intelligent and skilled.

No offense to him.

"I like him," Romeo announces with a grin. "He adds good value." When I hesitate, he adds, "What? You don't like him? Is it because he tried to hit on Bella at the party? Jeremiah told me he didn't know she was yours…"

He pulls me back, laughing, as I move to storm out there and beat the shit out of him. Okay, that doesn't sound right, but that fucker! Not that I can blame him.

My woman is perfection.

When I step back into the room, Jag is laughing at something that Julianna is saying and Bella all but jumps into my arms.

I almost forget why I was going to murder that bastard.

Almost.

"You didn't tell me Jag tried to hit on you?" I say gently, lifting my eyes and pinning him with my stare.

He puts his hands in the air. "I didn't know, River. And as soon as I did, trust me, I backed away. I just saw a pretty girl and tried to shoot my shot. You can't blame me."

"It's true," Bella says, pulling me away from Jag and down the hallway. "He didn't do anything wrong."

"He should know better," I growl.

She rolls her eyes and opens my bedroom door. "He does now."

The second we are locked inside, I wrap her in my arms and kiss her. She sighs contentedly, "I love you, River."

"I love you, too," I say, looking her in the eyes, so she knows how much I mean it. "I love you so much." I pick her up and lay her back on the black sheets. "Let me show you just how much."

I don't know how she got into my icy cold heart, but when I do love, it's with an intensity that might scare some.

But not her.

She was made for me.

Chapter Thirteen

Bella

"Hello, Bella speaking," I answer the phone, inwardly sighing when it's the city calling about the Lansdale property.

I was so excited about this property, but it's soon turning into the bane of my existence, even without the Rosalind issue, and I don't even know why our old MC president, Julianna's father, Paulie, was so adamant that we have it, or what he wants to use it for. I hope they didn't realize the signature was forged.

"I see—no, we don't have any permits in the works yet," I say, rolling my eyes.

We end the call and then I get another one straight after, asking how much I'm offering for an Angels property that just went on sale. Before I let the agent go, I ask about a two-acre estate he currently has listed. Romeo told me he wants to turn it into a massive joint clubhouse one day, and I can see why. It has everything: plenty of rooms, bathrooms, basketball court, a pool. And most importantly, it's secure, with big-ass gates around it on a large property. The clubhouses are nice now, but this would be next-level, and it would bring the two MCs together to live permanently. It's a big move, but one that might pay off if he plays it right.

"We will pay two million. Cash," I tell the real estate agent, which is five hundred thousand under the asking price and a million less than what Romeo gave me for a budget.

"We will get back to you," he says, but let's be real, they are going to accept the offer, because they know we are good for it and it will be an easy sale. And as if we don't know that they price houses up so there's room to negotiate? Come on now.

At the end of the day, the last person I expect to see waiting for me outside my work is none other than Mark.

Furious, I storm over to his car and scowl into the open window. "What the hell are you doing here?" I ask. "Come to tell me about your honeymoon or something? Can't you stalk your new woman instead?"

"Get in the car, Bella. I need to talk to you about something important," he says, his usual jovial demeanor missing. Instead, he's all business, with a very serious glint in his eyes.

I glance around the almost empty lot and hesitate.

So he does something that shocks the hell out of me. He pulls out a fucking badge and flashes it at me.

"Bullshit," I whisper, staring down at it. Mark is an FBI agent? Anger that I've never felt before fills my body. "Is this a fucking joke?"

"Get in the car," he growls, keeping his voice low.

I'd never once thought that Mark would be the kind of guy to hurt me, but I don't know what to think right now. In the end, though, curiosity wins, and I walk around and get into the car. I have so many questions, and my fingers are trembling with anxiety.

"Please tell me you only became an agent after we broke up," I say, staring straight ahead. "Tell me!"

"Bella—"

I slam my fists down on the dashboard. "Was it all a lie?"

"Let's go to some place where we can talk privately."

We sit in silence as Mark drives, and we end up at River's lake spot. The place he took me on the first night we met. The irony is not lost on me.

Mark turns the engine off and turns to me. "I'm sure you have a lot of questions."

"Oh, you best believe it."

He holds his hands up in surrender. "I get it. Let me go first. I was assigned to investigate the Angels properties. I'm in white-collar crime at the FBI and the government takes notice when a motorcycle club goes from having about twenty million dollars' worth of properties to over two hundred and fifty million dollars' worth in less than ten years."

Goddamn you, Julianna, for being too goddamn good at your job.

"Originally Julianna was the mark. She was the one I was supposed to get close to. But I met you by accident." I give him a look, knowing nothing can be an accident when he's been searching into my family. "Okay, well, I was at the bar you and she used to like to go to and I was sitting waiting for her when you came in and ordered a drink. There was something honest about you. And, well, you know what happened. I bought you a drink and you turned it down and then we sat three seats apart just talking. And that's when I knew I had a genuine connection with you, so I went to my boss and changed the plan."

"Lucky me," I say, the sarcasm dripping from my voice. "We dated for a fucking year, Mark. One year. What did you do? Go through my things when I was asleep? Spy on me?"

He has the decency to look offended. "What? No!"

He played me.

And he was actually more badass in real life than the character I was fucking dating.

"You proposed to me," I whisper. "Was any of it real? And why are you telling me now?"

"I don't have time to get into this now, I tried talking to you about it at your house," he explains, and when I finally turn and look at him I see some pain and regret flash in his eyes. "I'm sorry, okay, but I did have feelings for you."

"Save me the bullshit. Why?" I ask him, even though I already know the damn answer. He wanted information on the Angels MC. And he used me to get it. And you know what the messed-up part is? I trusted him enough that I did speak openly with him about a few things. Things he can now use against me and the club. Not-so-legal things he knows about that have my signature on them and might implicate me. "You know what, I know why. Just tell me why you're telling me now and what kind of shit I'm in."

"Yes, I was building a case for the feds," he admits, a muscle working in his jaw. "And then you broke up with me, which kind of ruined everything."

"Oh, I'm sorry!" I snap, my tone sarcastic and salty. "That must have been very inconvenient for you—"

"Bella. Fucking stop," he says in a voice he never once used with me. I need to wrap my head around the fact that the man I thought I knew is a fake. A facade. I also need to remember that I need to keep my mouth shut.

"You're not asking the right questions. Don't you want to know why it went on for a year with nothing?" I don't say anything. "You were clean. Everything, you and Julianna and the real estate operations. They were clean. It's why I got to stay with you for a year. The reason I proposed was because our operation was ending. I figured we could be free to be together."

I refuse to say anything. Did he really think I'd never find out? I'm so proud of past me for turning down that proposal. I knew there was something off, even if it was just that he was boring.

"The operation was closed. I was putting in my final report. Until…"

I hold my breath because I know what he is going to say.

"Lansdale."

Fuck you, Rosalind. But fuck me for being irresponsible and getting caught up with River instead of focusing on the paperwork.

"I can tell by your face that you know exactly what I'm talking about. A forged signature. That has many legal ramifications for the Angels. Not only federal, but local charges as well. So I'm here to offer you a deal," he says, studying me.

"What deal?" I whisper-yell. "This is my family you're talking about, Mark. I can't believe you did this to me."

"You could work with us for immunity," he suggests, shrugging casually like the bastard hasn't been planning this speech word for word. "All we need to know is who killed Victor Peterson."

I pause, frowning. "I don't know in what world you live in, but the Lansdale property and Victor have nothing to do with one another."

"Yes, but it's called leverage. Bella, I can put you away for a long time and do a thorough investigation into the Angels' business dealings. However, I could look away, if you help us."

"Look, let's assume I know what you're saying about the Lansdale property, which I do not. I don't know what happened to Victor, so I don't know how to help you," I say with the confidence Julianna would have, but me? I'm shitting my pants. Why the fuck do I need to know that River killed Victor? Why did Julianna tell me that? I could've really been blissfully ignorant.

"Find out. Let me know, and your little forgery stint will fly under the rug," he says, resting his arm on the steering wheel. I hate that it's an attractive pose. Where was this guy when we were dating?

Focus, Bella. Mark is lying scum and wants to hurt you and your family.

Pursing my lips, I wonder how the hell I'm going to get out of this one. "So basically, you're blackmailing me to do your job for you."

And this is after he tricked me into thinking he loved me and wanted to marry me.

Wow.

"Call it what you want. I'll give you a week or so and then come speak to you. Hopefully you'll have the information we need," he replies without any emotion. With that he starts the car and takes me back to my car.

When we get to the parking lot, I open the door, but then pause and turn back to him. "Did you even get married to someone else, or was that a lie, too?"

He stays quiet, so I get out and slam the door, and get into my own car and drive home.

Shit, what should I do?

I decide my best way of dealing with this is to speak to River and Romeo, so they can come up with a plan with me. I should also include Julianna. I could not tell them and try to deal with this on my own, but I've watched enough movies and read enough books to know that just telling them will save me time and a shitload of unnecessary drama.

That's the best thing to do, right?

Even if it means looking like an idiot.

Just fucking wonderful.

Chapter Fourteen

River

I don't know how to feel when I'm told that Bella got into a man's car in front of her workplace, but what I do is track down the car to see what the fuck this Mark is doing snooping around my woman. I wouldn't peg Bella for a cheater, or a person with weak character, but you never know these days. Did she get sick of my shit and go back with her ex?

I know I need to let her in more, but it's been really hard for me. Fuck.

Bella calls me but I'll have to call her back, as I'm a little bit busy stalking her ex. The first red flag is when he stops at the police station. The second is when the cops greet him like they know him.

Motherfucker.

Is he a cop?

No, I don't get those vibes from him. I send Jag a text with all the information I have on this Mark and ask him to do a background check. Fifteen minutes pass before I get a reply.

Jag: Not a cop, he's a fed.

I have so many questions, and only one beautiful, potentially devious woman is going to be able to answer them.

Does she know he's a fed? Is she working with them?

This would be just my fucking luck.

My phone buzzes with a text message from the devil herself.

Bella: I need to talk to you and Romeo.

River: You okay?

Bella: I'm fine, at home. But something happened.

River: Coming to you. Now.

Bella: With Romeo?

River: Yes.

Okay, depending on how this goes, my heart is either going to be broken or she's about to tell me the truth of why the fuck she got into the car of her fed ex-boyfriend.

Yeah, good luck explaining that one to Romeo.

When I call him, he must be balls-deep in his wife because he sounds pissed. "What? This better be important."

"I need you to come with me to Bella's—she's requested you there. No idea what's going on, but I just found out her ex-boyfriend is a fed."

I wince at all the cursing and end the call.

The rumbles of our motorcycles pull up to her place twenty minutes later, and the stomping of our large biker boots walking to her front door.

"This better be good," Romeo mutters.

I agree.

I want some answers, and I want them now.

"Hey." Bella smiles nervously as she opens the door wide for us to enter. She looks beautiful, still in her fancy businesswear. And I want nothing more than to tear that blouse off her. "Come in. Do you mind coming out to see my garden outside?"

Romeo looks at me with confusion, but we both follow her outside, Hades doing the same.

We take a seat on the outdoor bench and decline her offer of a drink. We just want to get straight to the point.

"What's going on?" Romeo asks, tapping his fingers on his leg with impatience.

She winces. "Okay, so after work today, my ex-boyfriend Mark was there waiting in his car for me." Her gray eyes are pinned on me. "You know, the one who showed up to my house recently? Yeah, him."

Romeo looks like he wants to throttle us both.

Bella continues, "Apparently he's an FBI agent and was only dating me to get information and dirt on my family and the MC." She looks at Romeo, reading the room. "I didn't know," she stammers. "I never knew. I thought he was some stupid accountant. He was so boring and I almost wish I knew because maybe the real him would've kept me interested—"

"Bella…" I say sternly. I do not need to hear this shit about her being turned on by an authoritative federal agent.

She looks at me with wide eyes. "Shit, yes, sorry. I didn't mean that. I'm still processing. I just meant—"

"Bella, tell me what he said and why I'm here," Romeo says in his president voice. It's one he usually only uses with the men.

She looks at him, a bit of fear in her gaze. "Right, sorry. Okay, well, recently, we were closing on this property. The Lansdale property."

Romeo nods. "I saw the report. It was something Paulie wanted, and we finally were able to buy it at the right price. What does that have to do with this?"

"Let her fucking finish," I say, warning him to not bite her head off.

"Yeah. Okay. Um…well, so there was a very strict deadline on closing and the paperwork didn't get finalized correctly—"

"Why is that?" Romeo tries to ask nicely but it's coming out as annoyance.

"That was the same day I walked in on you in the garage…so I was distracted. I, uh, wasn't focused at work and when I left for the day I forgot to sign the documents. Sally, our new assistant, called all the Callistos since any one of us could sign it and, well, she got Rosalind…"

Romeo groans. Rosalind has been a touchy subject because Romeo used to sleep with her before he met Julianna, who happens to be her sister. I thought they patched things up, but family gatherings are definitely awkward as hell. Although now that I know what I know about my mother and Andrew, I guess awkward relationships run in the family.

Bella continues, "Rosalind signed my name. I don't know why. When I confronted her, she told me to thank her for saving my ass."

Romeo rubs his face with his hands. "Fuck me. Okay, so you're saying you closed on the Lansdale property with forged documents."

Bella nods. I personally don't see what the big deal is here. It's not like she embezzled money. It was a fucking clerical error. What the fuck do the feds think they could do with that? "And he says that he can prosecute me for forgery and open an entire investigation and audit of the Angels real estate dealings because of it."

"Unless…?" Romeo says, knowing what is coming next.

Bella sighs. "Unless I give them information on what happened to Victor."

And there it is. They're going to use a false signature to get us for murder.

"But you don't know anything about Victor," I say, because it's not like we talk about that shit post-sex.

She bites her lip and refuses to look at me. "Julianna told you, didn't she?" Romeo says.

Oh fuck. She knows? She knows what I'm capable of? And she's still with me? There are too many thoughts going through my head right now.

Romeo and I share a look.

"What exactly do you know?" Romeo asks.

She still refuses to look at me. "I don't know much. Just that you let River…do it." She manages to get it out and then finally looks me in the eye.

"First of all, thank you for telling us this, Bella. I appreciate it, and it makes our job much easier trying to fix it," Romeo says.

I couldn't agree more. I'm so proud that she came right to us and didn't drag this out or make it worse by not telling us the truth.

"Second, is that why you brought us outside? In case Mark's bugged your house?"

She nods. That's my girl. Always thinking.

"Tell us more about this forgery situation," I ask.

"There isn't anything more. It's never happened before. But I saw the signature. It looks nothing like mine and if anyone were to look closer, they'd see it."

"You said any Callisto could've signed that paperwork. Why did Rosalind sign your name?" I ask, feeling like I'm missing a piece of the puzzle here.

She shrugs. "Why does Rosalind do anything? Because she can."

"Does he have any evidence?" I ask, jaw tight as ever.

"The paperwork is public record. If it comes out the Angels will be audited, and while we run a clean business, you know not every business is a hundred percent clean, especially when there is an MC behind it. And besides that, it can jeopardize not only the Lansdale deal but all our pending transactions, like the property you wanted me to offer on for the new clubhouse. Agents in town will not want to work with us if we have a history of forgery," she says, and I realize the full scope of this. This puts everything the Angels have built in jeopardy. "I'm so sorry that I've brought these problems to our doors. I honestly had no clue that he was a fed. And I know how stupid that makes me look."

"Look, it's not your fault. You had no control over the situation," I quickly say, frowning. "And this Mark, he has bigger problems than finding Victor now. And I don't want you alone here. Can't you work from home? You can stay at the clubhouse."

"Yeah, I suppose I can. I don't think Julianna would care. Oh, Julianna!" She looks at Romeo. "I have to tell her, don't I?"

Romeo nods. "Yeah, I can't keep this from her. Not only is it club business, but it's you. It's Rosalind. She needs to know."

"She's going to be so disappointed in me." She hangs her head.

"No, you did nothing wr—" I'm about to finish

my sentence when Romeo gives me a glare, telling me to stop talking. He does blame her. I stand up and offer her my hand. "Come on, pack a bag. I'm taking you and Hades back with me."

Hades tilts his head to the side, then gets up from his outdoor bed, as if agreeing with me.

The ride back to the clubhouse is quiet, except for Hades's heavy breathing, and I think we both feel an impending sense of doom. I feel bad for ever questioning her. My initial gut feeling was right, she is a good woman. And I'm never going to question that again.

I make sure she's comfortable and then head off with Romeo.

We have a fed to deal with.

I've never wanted to beat the shit out of someone more in my life.

"That's him there," I say, later that day, nodding to the man leaving the police station and getting into his silver car. "And that's the car I've seen following me recently."

"Shit," Romeo mutters, pushing his sunglasses up on his nose. "I just want to know why they suddenly want to find out what happened to Victor. What's it to them?"

"They are not going to find him," I reply in a dry tone.

"Exactly, no evidence can be tied back to us. That's why they need Bella to do their dirty work for them," he says. As Mark drives off, we follow behind him at a safe distance. "She's never done anything criminal before, I don't know if his threats are even valid, but we don't want to risk it either. There is a lot at stake if they decide to make this forged signature a big deal."

"Agreed. I think we should find something on him in return, or just teach him a lesson," I say, cracking my knuckles to emphasize my point. "He's fucked with the wrong person."

No one messes with my Bella.

No one.

"Just don't do anything until we come up with a plan," Romeo states, knowing my impulsive nature. "We need to play it smart because the last thing we want is more feds on our ass. And that includes not touching him."

"I know." But to be honest, I probably needed the reminder.

"This could be his house," Romeo comments as we watch Mark enter a suburban property. We park across the road and wait for any movement.

After an hour, he comes out in a fresh change of clothes, so we guess this is indeed his residence. We keep following up, until Jag and Jeremiah come and swap with us so we can head back to the clubhouse. We are going to keep eyes on him until we find something out that we can use to our advantage.

When I get back, Bella is in the kitchen with Julianna. The two must've discussed what happened. Things must be okay because I spot the two of them cooking and singing along to old-school tracks by the likes of Whitney Houston and the Spice Girls. I watch Bella for a moment, swaying to the beat as she stirs whatever she has on the stove, before I let my presence be known.

"You're back," she says, spinning around. Hades is at her feet. I couldn't bring her here without also bringing her sidekick. "We're making a large pot of pasta for everyone."

"I can see that—it smells good," I say, giving her a kiss.

"Where's Romeo?" Julianna asks.

"He's out front. I think he's on a phone call," I say, and Julianna leaves to find him. "Things seem… good between you two. Did you talk?" I ask Bella. She's not my Bella yet. She's fidgety and on edge. Even her kisses feel off.

She nods. "We did. She was upset with me for not coming to her, for not focusing on work."

"That's unfair, you couldn't have known—"

Bella holds her hand up to me. "Don't do that. I don't need you sugarcoating what I did or telling me it wasn't a big deal. It was a major fuckup and I dropped the ball. Twice. First by missing the deadline and not signing the paperwork and second after learning of the issue and not doing anything to rectify it. I put a lot of people at risk here and while it might not be a big deal to you, please do not justify anything I did."

"But Rosalind…" I start, trying to wrap my arms around her.

She moves away and turns to me. "River, do you not see that this was my fault? Sure, Rosalind screwed me by signing my name, but if it wasn't for me, she never would've been needed. I dropped the ball. I was too preoccupied with what I saw in the garage and wondering if you and I were right for each other…"

What. The. Fuck.

"Whether we're right for each other?" I say, my hackles rising.

She sighs. "River, you don't talk to me. You tell me nothing about anything. We don't know each other's parents, we don't do anything other than hang out and fuck. You keep me at arm's length. Christ, I found out about Victor from Julianna! And that day I walked in the garage, I saw you beating a man to a pulp. I knew. And looking back, I don't think I really cared. Not about the blood or what you were doing in there. I cared more about the fact that you were hiding it from me. That you were hiding yourself from me."

I don't know what to say. I've been a fool. Maybe she's right. We've been living in this bubble where we are tiptoeing around the real conversations that need to be had. Everyone has been warning me about this, but fuck. I didn't realize Bella felt the same.

She caresses my face. "The fact that you are trying to convince me this is not my fault makes me love you, but that's not the support I need. I need someone who will let me hold myself accountable. Who will not sugarcoat things. I need you to not blame anyone but me."

I grunt. "I do blame Mark. And I can fucking blame Rosalind, too."

She nods with a smile. "Sure, they're both complicit. But I need you to show me how you feel about what I did."

My eyes widen. "To be honest, I really don't think what you did was that big of a deal. I've done worse shit," I say with honesty.

She laughs. "Okay. Fair. I appreciate that. But don't let me talk myself out of my own guilt. Don't do that. I don't need a savior or a knight in shining armor, River. I need a partner. One who will help me up when I fall."

I kiss her, and this time she allows me to. "Do you honestly think we're not good for one another?"

She bites her lip and then nods. "I don't know who you are. You won't let me."

As much as I want to tell her she's wrong, I know she is right. "So what do we have to do to see if we're right for one another?" I ask.

"This is a great first start," she says.

Romeo and Julianna come in and things are a bit awkward. Julianna's youngest sister, Veronica, joins us all for dinner. The two of them have been working on their relationship after not being very close. In fact, Veronica used to sleep with Victor while he was betrothed to Julianna, and Julianna didn't even know. But you can imagine the drama.

I notice that Bella isn't too close with Veronica either, even though she is also her cousin, and obviously feels more comfortable with Julianna, openly engaging with her. Bella and Corey get along so well, which is important for me. Whoever loves me has to love my sister. Everyone just assumes I'm overprotective because she's beautiful, and I don't want any men near her. And while that is all true, I'm protective of her because I've looked after her for her whole life. She's been with me through everything, and I always made sure she was kept safe from Robert. I never liked leaving her alone with him. And now apparently I don't like leaving her alone with any other man either.

After dinner we all help clean up and the women go to watch a movie together in the theater room while Romeo and I speak to Jag and Jeremiah, who have let us know that Mark has retired for the night. So now we know where he lives, but not much else. Bringing down the MC has obviously been a long-term investment for him, but asking Bella to get him information seems like a desperate attempt, so I don't think he has anything other than Bella's fake signature.

And I'm betting he doesn't want Bella to go to prison. He's just using whatever he can to manipulate her, not thinking that she'd tell anyone about it.

I'm so proud of her for trusting me and messaging

me right away about it. That's why I didn't want to lose my shit on her stupid ex-boyfriend, because she needs to be able to come to me at all times.

I've just gotten out of the shower when Bella steps into the room, and I don't miss her eyes trailing down my bare chest and to where my towel is sitting on my hips.

"Like something you see?" I ask in a husky tone.

She smiles widely and locks the door behind her. "I can't help it that you look so good." She steps closer and runs her fingers down my abs, tracing each muscle. "You are seriously so sexy."

"Pretty sure that's my line." I grin, grabbing her by her waist and bringing her up against me. "You are so beautiful," I say, kissing her. "Gorgeous." Another kiss. "Sexy." A deeper, lingering kiss this time. "And mine," I finally say against her sweet lips. "All fucking mine."

My towel drops, and so does her gaze.

I help her take off her clothes, and then hook a finger in her black panties, using them to lead her to the bed.

And then she loses those, too.

She crawls onto the bed playfully, giving me a nice show as she bends over. I get on the bed to chase after her, pinning her down and rolling her over, and kissing her, pouring emotion into it.

"I love you," she says.

"I love you, too."

I'm fucking obsessed with her.

And I mean that in the very best way.

I kiss down her body, gently spread her thighs and make her come with my mouth. I love the taste of her, her scent and the little noises she makes. There's not one thing I don't like about her.

And when I slide into her sweet pussy, it's like coming home. She wraps her legs around me and lifts her hips up to every thrust, the already satisfied expression on her face making me even harder.

"River," she moans, kissing my neck and gently biting down on my skin. I pin her arms back above her head and lower my face to her breasts, kissing and licking her nipples until she's moaning in pleasure.

Only when she's come once more do I let myself finish.

And then she straddles me and just lies there on top of me with my arms wrapped around her tightly. "Tell me something no one else knows," she says as she catches her breath.

I'm silent for a while thinking about what I could tell her. "I sometimes wish Victor had killed me instead of Matthew."

She sits up to look at me. Really look at me.

"I'm glad he didn't," she says before kissing me.

"Matthew was so good, so full of life. He had so much promise. He should still be alive. I'd gladly take his place if I could."

She lets me talk about Matthew, something I haven't

done in a while with anyone. And then we fall asleep entwined together.

I don't know what I did to deserve such a good life, but I'm going to do everything in my power to keep it.

Chapter Fifteen

Bella

I wake up naked, with some coffee, pancakes and a letter next to my bed.

Gone with Romeo.
    Message me if you need anything, or Jag is there—he can go get whatever you need.
See you this evening,
Love, River

Smiling, I sit up and eat my breakfast before getting in the shower. I take my time, washing my hair and shaving, apparently not in a rush this morning. It's 9 AM by the time I'm ready to leave the bedroom. I take my laptop with me and sit outside in the sunshine with Hades doing zoomies around the garden, while I answer some work emails and catch up on life administration.

I notice Jag open the sliding door and pop his head out. "You need anything?" he asks.

"No, I'm okay. Is Julianna still here?" I ask.

"No, she went to run some errands and do some grocery shopping for the clubhouse," he explains, coming outside and sitting next to me. "Jeremiah is with her—can never be too careful."

"You're not upset you're stuck here with me?" I ask, using my hands to shield the sun so I can see his face.

He shakes his head. "No, of course not. I do what's needed to help out. The fact that River trusts me to stay with you means a lot to me too, especially after Romeo told him that I tried hitting on you. So he obviously knows I find you attractive, but he trusts me to act right."

"It really wasn't that big of a deal," I assure him.

He smiles sheepishly. "Thanks. Let me know if you want to go anywhere or need anything. I'm going to be in the gym getting a workout in."

"Okay, sounds good."

He disappears and I finish up my work until it's lunchtime, then I wander inside, where Jeremiah is carrying in bags and bags of food. I help him unload it all and smile when I notice that Julianna has stocked all my favorite snacks and drinks.

"She's so sweet," I comment.

"River told her to get everything you like—he gave her his credit card and said to buy whatever," Jeremiah says, placing the pack of bottled water in the fridge. "I don't think that man could say no to you if he tried."

I mean, how could I not love that man?

He definitely spoils me.

My phone beeps. Could he sense I was thinking about him?

But unfortunately, it's not River at all.

Mark: You got any information on Victor yet?

Fucking Mark.

I send River a text, keeping him updated.

"Hey," Corey says, stepping into the kitchen with bags full of shopping. "I did a little retail therapy and you're the only woman here right now so I'm going to need to show you everything."

I put down my phone to give her my full attention. "Okay, let's move to the living room so I can get comfortable."

Once I'm sitting on the couch, she starts showing me all her purchases: new jeans and tops, dresses and sneakers. She has good taste, and everything is really cute.

"Is there an occasion for this?" I ask, inspecting the items.

She puts the shoebox back in the bag. "Not really. Matthew…" She trails off. "He had a lot of money in his bank account when he died, and River gave half to me and half to our mom. And I rarely spend any of it, so I thought I'd treat myself. More as a distraction than anything."

"Do you see your mom?" I ask, and she shakes her head.

"Not since Matthew died. We had a big fight and it was kind of a bad one. She blamed me," she says, swallowing hard. "Apparently I shouldn't have been out in the first place, and I'm the one who got him into the fight. She told me it was my fault. She lost her favorite child, so of course she blamed her least favorite child."

"It was no one's fault except Victor's," I say, frowning. "You did nothing wrong, you just happened to be there the night it happened." Unlike me, Corey really was just an innocent bystander.

"I know," she replies, smiling sadly. "She just needed someone to blame. River still sees our mom. He asks me to go with him sometimes, but I'm not ready just yet. She's been through a lot, so I know he feels bad for her. You know River, he has a hero complex. He wants to save everyone."

I've never thought of it like that, probably because most people are scared of River and he's not known as a people person, but I can see how he would appear like that to his baby sister.

"I saw you chatting with Damon at the party— what was that all about?" I tease, lightening the mood with a change of subject.

She rolls her eyes, but I don't miss the sudden flush in her cheeks. "I don't even know—that was my first time seeing him. He's obviously hot, and I'm guessing used to women falling at his feet, so I wasn't going to give him that satisfaction. I called him a short king to humble him—he told me he's over six feet, so I said oh, sorry, it doesn't look like you are. I suppose it's gaslighting, isn't it?"

I burst out laughing. "A short king? Oh my God, he would have loved that one."

"Yeah, it works on all men; they have such fragile egos. Not that there's anything wrong with short men," she adds quickly. "I just don't have time or the space to have my heart broken any further."

"That's very insightful of you," I say, helping her pack up the rest of her shopping items. "And you know if you ever need anything, I'm here for you. No judgment."

She smiles. "Thanks, Bella. I'm glad that River has you. It means I don't have to worry about him anymore. Because he's your problem."

I laugh. "Yes, I guess he is. And I'm his."

"I always wanted a sister," she adds, hazel eyes lighting up in a childlike way. "Maybe I lost a sibling, but I'll also gain one."

"Okay, you're going to make me cry if you don't stop," I say, clearing my throat.

She stands up, grabbing all her bags with her. "I'm going to put this stuff away in my room. Thanks for the chat."

"Anytime," I call out as she leaves.

My mind roams back to Mark's message, and when

Julianna returns from running errands, I bring it up with her.

"How should I reply?" I ask. "Do I want him to think I'm helping him? I think that buys some more time."

We had a very long discussion before Romeo and River came home yesterday. I could tell how disappointed she was in me. But like I said to River, I own my mistakes. I refuse to leave the blame on anyone but myself and I think she appreciates that.

"Yeah, I think you should just reply saying that you're asking around and trying to see what everyone knows, or something. You have to play the game, too," she says. "If you ignore him, he'll probably discount the idea of you helping, and who knows what his next move will be."

Bella: I'm seeing what I can find out. You said I had a week.

I read it out loud to her before I hit Send.

"Yeah, that's good. God, he's such an asshole," she adds, shaking her head. "Little weasel. Was he good in bed at least? He better have been for all the shit you have to deal with when it comes to him."

"I thought he was, but after being with River…he pales in comparison," I reply quietly, and the two of us are giggling together when River himself walks in with Romeo.

"What are you two up to?" he asks, amused.

"Nothing much, Mark texted me so we were talking about that."

"What did he ask?" Romeo asks before River can, going into president mode.

I show them both my phone. "Seems desperate for this information. I wonder what's on the line for him."

"I don't know. Maybe his job? Maybe he has to come up with something for all his time undercover?" I suggest, wincing when I realize *I* was his undercover job.

He was under some covers all right.

Not a bad job to have, even finish the night off with an orgasm on top of his salary.

"We need to find something on him quickly," River growls, good mood disappearing. "I don't like that he's messaging you."

"I don't like it either, but I need to buy us the time to figure this out," I say.

I don't want to go to prison, and I don't want anyone to get into trouble for me either.

Basically I need Mark to leave me and the club the hell alone.

Chapter Sixteen

River

While Bella and Julianna go out for brunch the next day, with Jag and Jeremiah keeping an eye on them, I decide to do a quick bedroom makeover, turning the empty room next to it into an office. I buy a new desk, chair and daybed, along with a mini fridge stocked with drinks, water and snacks. I clean it all up and make it look perfect. I might not know much about interior decorating, but the room looks peaceful and inviting and I hope Bella likes it.

"That looks amazing, River," Corey comments as she walks past. She leans against me and studies the room in awe. "You even added plants. I love it."

"Thanks," I reply, smiling down at her. "I want Bella to feel at home here and have her own space."

"Who knew you could be so sweet?" Corey teases, nudging me with her elbow. "She's lucky to have you."

"Now you're being sweet," I mutter.

"Are you going to take her to meet Mom? Bella was asking about her yesterday," she says, still gazing out at the new office. "I think you should take her. You two have been together long enough to meet the parents, don't you think?"

I nod. "Yeah, I know. It's just complicated, isn't it? I don't like talking about… Dad. And I know all of that is going to come up when she sees Mom and asks about what happened to her eye. I don't know. I don't like to think about him at all."

Even though he's not biologically my father, he's still the one who raised me. The asshole is still a part of me, whether I like it or not.

"He is not who you are," she says quietly. "But it is your past, and I think sharing that might bring you even closer. I mean, what do I know, I haven't even had a proper boyfriend before, but I do know that Bella would never judge you. She loves you."

I wrap my arm around Corey and she rests her head on my shoulder. "Yeah, you're right. Sometimes it's easier said than done. I'm doing so well just ignoring it, you know?"

She laughs. "You're such a typical male. Now while you're in a good mood and we're having a deep and meaningful chat, I should probably let you know that I'm taking some time off from college."

"Corey—" My first thought is to tell her no. But she didn't ask permission. That she's making a mistake and needs to stay in school. But I know she's still grieving, and if that's what she needs to do, I should support her.

"Not forever, but my head's not in it right now, and I need a break. I knew you wouldn't like it, but it's my life and I need some time to just... I don't know. Find myself."

She's right, I don't like it. Her getting an education was very important for me, but yeah, it is her life.

"Okay, if that's what you want to do," I say with a sigh.

"Really?" she asks, eyes going wide. "That's it? Wow, Bella has made you soft."

"It's your life and I want you to be happy. I know you've been struggling, Corey. All I want is for you to be how you were before we lost Matthew. College isn't going anywhere."

She fiddles with the sleeves of her sweater and her habit is a dark, unsaid cloud. "I don't do it anymore— it just made me feel better at the time. I wasn't coping well when we lost him. Going to therapy helps."

"I know," I admit, smiling sadly. "And the pain will never fully go away, I think we just learn to carry it with us better."

"You're all I have left, you know that? I mean, you and Mom, but our relationship has always struggled. I think she liked having sons more than she liked having a daughter."

"Maybe one day you two will work it out, whenever you're ready for that. But until then you have me, and I'm not going anywhere," I promise her.

She hugs me tighter. "I love you, brother. But it would be nice if you stopped chasing away any men who want to date me, because I don't want to be a virgin forever."

I wince. "I don't know what you're talking about. You were chatting with Damon at the party and I didn't do anything."

"Yeah, because of Bella. And wow, everyone has commented on Damon. You know, I can have a conversation with someone with a penis and it doesn't have to mean anything. I'm used to being around bikers my whole life, it's not unusual for me," she says, rolling her eyes.

She is being a little too defensive on the Damon subject, but I'm smart enough to not point that out. "You have all the time in the world to date, and you said you want to find yourself first, so do that," I suggest, turning my head when I hear a door open. "I think they are home."

I close the office door and walk up the hallway, Corey at my side. I hear them before I see them.

"I can't wait to get drunk when I'm not pregnant anymore," Julianna says.

Bella laughs. "You know you can't drink when you're breastfeeding either."

"Oh yeah. Can you get pregnant, too? Misery loves company."

More laughter.

"Hey." Bella smiles widely as she sees me. "You missed out on an epic brunch—the food was so good."

"What a shame that I missed out on all that pregnancy chat," I reply, grinning.

Bella rolls her eyes. "We did talk about other things."

I lead her to the office and open the door. "I have a surprise for you."

She glances up at me in confusion before stepping inside, her gaze widening as she takes it all in.

"Your new office. I even stocked the fridge for you. And now you have your own space if it gets too much here," I say, shifting on my feet as she walks around touching everything.

When she turns around, there are tears in her eyes. "I think this is the nicest thing anyone has done for me," she says, lips trembling. "I love it so much, River. Thank you. All the little touches are so me, and shows just how much you know me."

She runs back and gives me the best hug. "You're welcome."

"And I love the daybed, it's so pretty." She continues on, complimenting every detail, and being so appreciative that I just want to give her a whole fucking house next time.

Maybe I will.

I pat Hades, who comes in to explore his new place to nap, while Bella makes herself comfortable. She calls Julianna over and shows off her new office, while I stand at the door watching her with a smile on my face. I don't remember a time in my

life that I've been this happy, my scowl lines turning into smile lines.

What has she done to me?

If only Robert, that bastard, could see me now.

He didn't break me at all.

And I'm only just realizing.

Chapter Seventeen

Bella

Romeo, River and a few of the other men head off to do biker stuff, and I enjoy working in my new office. I didn't think I could love River any more, but the effort he put into this was so sweet, down to the fridge filled with my favorite sodas and chocolates. He notices everything and obviously listens when I speak, because he nailed it all. He even stocked up on all of Hades's favorite treats. How cute is that?

I feel special as fuck and I love it. River has this bad reputation as being the darkest brother in the MC, and now that I have seen that side of him too, I love him even more. I see the protector. The one who will do whatever it takes to protect those he loves. I know that it's there, underneath, but I also know he would never hurt me. I trust him one hundred percent.

Mark finally replies to my text.

Mark: Time is running out.

Bella: Maybe if you explain what's on the line I can try to understand what's going on here?

Mark: You don't understand? Just do as I'm asking. I need some evidence to take down Romeo Montanna.

I see.
So he wants to take down Romeo, and thinks that Victor is the key to doing so?

Bella: I don't want to give evidence that's made up. I'm already in enough trouble.

Mark: So you're saying Romeo didn't kill Victor?

Shit. I shouldn't be doing this.

Bella: I'm saying I don't know what happened. I actually do not know. Victor could've just left the country. He had a lot of enemies. If the FBI can't figure it out, how am I supposed to?

Mark: You are one of them. Snoop around.

Bella: You think they tell the women everything?

Mark: Bella. It's important.

Bella: What have you gotten yourself into?

He doesn't reply, but it makes me think I might be on to something. Maybe he'll tell me the truth and we can figure out what is going on here.

When River gets home that night, I ask him if our resident tech guru, Jag, can hack into Mark's cell, and tell him about the conversation I had with him via text today.

"One step ahead of you," he replies, and explains that they bugged Mark's car today and that Jag is currently trying to hack into his phone line and home security.

"I wonder what we're going to find," I murmur, pulling down the sheets and sliding into the bed. I haven't been home in a few days other than to grab some things, and I actually like staying here. Hades even seems to like it, with so many people to love on him every day. He's been sleeping on the couch and living his best life. He's slowly becoming the club mascot and doesn't have to spend the day at home alone while I'd be at work.

"I don't know, but don't stress. We'll find a way out of it, we always do," he assures me, stripping down to his birthday suit and getting in next to me. "I fucking love having you here in my bed every night. Our bed."

"And I love being here," I reply, turning to face him. I trace his jawline with my finger. "How things have changed—you went from not even letting me know where you were for days, to moving me in with you."

He laughs, blue eyes lighting up. "We have come a long way, haven't we? I need to take you to meet my mother. She asks about you every time I see her."

"I'd love that," I reply, feeling a little emotional that he's finally brought this up. "You can meet my parents as soon as they are back from their adventures." I don't know what they'd think about River, but I don't care. I'm sure that he's the man I want to be with, and no one could convince me otherwise.

"That sounds good," he says, kissing my forehead. "Are you happy staying here? If you want to go back to your house, we can. I don't want you to feel like you have to stay."

"I'm happy," I assure him. "And if that changes and I'm feeling homesick, I'll let you know. But I'm happy wherever you and Hades are. And now with my new office…wait, that was your plan all along, wasn't it? Get me all comfortable here with no need for me to go home."

"Did it work?" he asks, pulling me closer and kissing my neck.

"Yes, yes it did." I rest my head on his chest and his arms come around me. I'm almost asleep when there's a knock on the door.

"River?" It's Romeo.

River kisses me and tucks me in before jumping out of bed and throwing some shorts on, and then seeing what his president wants. Romeo speaks in a low tone, so I can't hear exactly what's been said, but it seems serious.

"I'll be back," River says, pressing his lips to the top of my head.

He gets dressed and leaves, and I wonder what the hell could be going on at eleven at night. I try to sleep, I do, but I'm wide awake at this point and I leave the room to go into the kitchen to make myself hot chocolate. Hades runs up to me and I pat him while heating up some water.

When I hear what sounds like a shout, I wonder if I'm imagining things. When I hear it a second time, I get up and go to investigate. The voice sounds familiar. Is someone in trouble? What is going on now? Is River here still or did he leave the clubhouse? My feet take me back to the infamous garage, which is where the voices are coming from. I know this didn't end so well for me last time, but I open the door anyway and step inside.

And there I see River.

Beating the shit out of Mark.

Romeo sees me and rushes me out of the garage, but not before I see River mercilessly pummeling Mark in the face and stomach, wearing an expression that I've never seen before.

He's in his element, almost.

I wince with every sickening sound. Why is he the one they always go to if violence is involved? Does he volunteer? Does he enjoy it?

I push Romeo off me and bolt back into the garage.

"River, what are you doing?" I call out, and he turns to look at me, letting go of Mark, who falls to the ground in a heap. River's eyes gentle as they land on me, the monster turning back into the man I know and love.

Romeo grabs me and pulls me away before River can say anything back to me.

"Why is Mark here?" I ask Romeo, who has me gently by the arm, leading me back to my bedroom.

"We found him outside, trying to look around," he explains, stopping at the door. "I know you are curious, but River wouldn't want you down there, so stay in bed until he gets back."

"He's punching the shit out of Mark! I can't just go to bed and act like everything is fine," I growl, pulling my arm away from him as the shock starts to wear off.

"He's blackmailing you, Bella. What did you think would happen if River got his hands on him? You aren't dating a gentle, timid man. River is... River," Romeo replies, studying me. "And you know this."

I feel bad for Mark, not that I'd tell River that, but I do. Yeah, he's an asshole, but I don't like to see anyone getting hurt like that. I take a few deep breaths, trying to calm myself down.

Romeo heads back down to the torture chamber and I go back into the kitchen, wondering what the hell I'm supposed to do right now. Do I try to stop him? Do I just let him do his thing and get information out of Mark? I really should have gone back to bed and pretended that I didn't hear anything.

I empty the water out of the kettle, suddenly not interested in a hot beverage, and get out a bottle of beer instead. After a few sips, I decide I can't just let this happen to Mark and storm back down to the garage. Only this time I walk right into River, the two of us stopping and staring at each other.

"What are you going to do with him?" I ask, my voice breathless.

"Why did you come down there?" he asks in return, shaking his head. "I never wanted you to see me like that again."

"But that side of you is a part of who you are," I state.

He nods slowly. "Yes, I guess it is. But not for you. Never for you."

"River, I know that."

And I do. I'm not scared of him.

Maybe I'm a little scared for other people, but I know he'd never hurt anyone he cares about.

"If you want to go home, I can take you, or I can get Jag to take you…"

"I'm not going anywhere," I reply, grabbing his arm and pulling him back to our room. "What happens now? With Mark, I mean."

"Well, you don't have to worry about him turning you in for the forgery. Mark was fired and has been trying to use Victor's crime to get his way back in. Not only that, but someone is blackmailing him to take down Romeo. I don't know who or why, but we will get to the bottom of it," he says, clearing his throat. "You need to listen sometimes, Bella. If I tell you to stay somewhere, it would be nice if you actually fucking stayed there."

I open the door and step into the bedroom. "I heard a noise, as if you wouldn't have done the same thing."

He sighs heavily and locks the door behind us. His knuckles are busted and instead of getting back into bed, he jumps in the shower, while I sit on the corner of the mattress trying not to think about Mark sitting in the garage, likely injured, unemployed and apparently blackmailed. I know I shouldn't feel bad, he's done nothing but lie and use me, but it's not like we can keep him down there forever. I trust River. I know he's just doing what he is supposed to. And I accept him for who he is. But does my first test of faith have to be with my ex-boyfriend?

I get back into bed, but sleep doesn't come.

Chapter Eighteen

River

I know I should have played it smarter, but when Romeo told me Mark was found creeping around our clubhouse, I just grabbed him and lost my shit. How dare he come here? He either has balls of fucking steel or no sense at all, and I'm thinking it's the latter.

He gave up the information pretty quickly, and knowing he doesn't work for the FBI anymore makes me feel better about what he has on Bella. I have a feeling there's more to this story, though, and he's not leaving until we get to the bottom of it.

Do I hate that Bella saw me hitting him?

Yes.

I wanted to hide that side of myself from her for as long as I could. It would kill me if she's scared, or thinks that I'm a monster.

She hasn't asked to leave, though, so maybe it

didn't scare her too much. Although she seemed too worried about her ex-boyfriend for my liking.

Fuck.

Is this being in love?

Overthinking every damn thing and constantly wondering if you're good enough?

Just fucking great.

If I were a better man, I would have left Bella well alone, but I'm not. She's in bed when I leave the bathroom, and I get in next to her. I'll deal with Mark tomorrow, and I'll figure out what the fuck we're going to do with him. But for now I should try to get some rest.

I don't know if I should hug her like I usually would, or if she's mad and doesn't want me to. Man, I hate this shit.

I slowly get closer to her, and when she doesn't move away or tell me to leave her alone, I pull her against my body, spooning her from behind, feeling relief that she's letting me. I don't know what I'd do if she ever decided to walk away from me.

I'd do anything to keep her.

When I wake up in the morning it's to an empty bed, and I have a moment of panic wondering if she left on her own and went home. I run out in my boxer shorts, but come to a stop when I see her in the kitchen with Julianna, having coffee, the two of them chatting among themselves.

"I heard you had a busy night," Julianna says when

she looks up and sees me standing there. "And nice of you to get dressed up for breakfast."

"Where's Romeo?" I ask, but my eyes are on Bella, who is now looking right back at me.

"He's with the prisoner. Still can't believe I slept through all that," Julianna grumbles, taking a sip from her mug. She then stands up and walks past me. "I hope you have a plan for the ex-boyfriend."

I don't, but thanks to her for pointing that out.

"Are you okay?" I ask Bella when we're alone. "I'm sorry about last night. I know it must have been scary for you and I should have handled the situation better."

She nods slowly. "It could have been handled better, yes. But I understand things work differently around here, and I just want the whole thing to be over with. Did I like seeing you hurt someone? No. Did I like seeing Mark get hurt? No. And not because I care about him or anything like that—I wouldn't want to see anyone I know get hit. I don't…enjoy seeing that stuff." She pauses, and then asks, "Do you? Because you looked like you were in your element."

I don't know how to answer that, because I'm not sure if I've ever admitted the truth about it, or even fully understand how I feel about it. "I do what needs to be done. That's my job as club enforcer."

"And you enjoy your job as club enforcer," she presses, and I don't know what she wants from me, but when I think about it honestly, yes, I do enjoy it.

"And if I do?"

"Then you're being honest," she replies, standing up and walking over to me. "I just wanted to hear you say it."

"And does that change anything for you? How you feel about it?" I ask, holding my breath as I wait for her reply.

She frowns. "I've spent a lot of time thinking about it, and struggling with it. But I know that you're a good man. To me, anyway, and to those you love. I see how you love those around you, how you love me. I know you're a complicated person, but I trust you. And I feel safe with you."

She hugs me tightly, and then goes back into our bedroom to get ready for the day.

Without knowing it, she's just given me the best gift ever.

Acceptance.

I've always thought I'd be seen as a monster, and no one, especially women, ever got to know the real me. I kept all of that hidden. But Bella is slowly seeing everything, and she's not running. In fact, she only seems to love me more. Corey was right.

I've really hit the jackpot with her. She's not just a woman I love.

She is *the* woman.

I get dressed and head down into the garage, where Romeo is sitting with Mark, who has been untied. Romeo's even given him some food and water, obviously onto the good cop routine. Mark freezes when he sees me, and the fear in his eyes is a familiar look.

"Someone has kidnapped Mark's fiancée," Romeo says to me, "and told him if he wants her back alive, he needs to bring me down."

Fuck. So he isn't married, but close enough.

"Same person who put out the hit on you? Was it a woman?" I ask Mark, who nods. "Is that how you found out about the forgery?"

"No, actually. I found the forgery by looking at public documents. I know Bella's signature and that the person who signed her name was definitely not her. I found it on dumb luck. But it *is* a woman who's blackmailing me," he replies, swallowing hard. "Now that I've told you both the truth, are you going to help me or not? I can't let anything happen to Sarah."

Shit.

We are up to our neck in our own problems, and now we're going to help the love of my life's ex-FBI agent ex find his fiancée? Oh, and our own grandmother, who we can't locate, might have her.

Wonderful.

Romeo looks over at me and I shrug. I mean, he did tell us the truth about everything. And we do want to find Cathy anyway.

But I don't trust this Mark guy one bit.

Romeo nods, as if he can read my mind and understand, and we've known each other so long he probably does. "We'll see what we can do. But we've already been looking for this person with no luck, so don't get too excited. And if you double-cross or betray us in any way, I will let River do whatever he wants to you."

Mark gulps and agrees to the terms.

So I guess that's what we're doing now.

Chapter Nineteen

Bella

"Wait, what?" I ask when River tells me about the new plan. "Someone kidnapped Mark's fiancée?" No wonder he went quiet when I asked him if he really was married to someone.

"Yeah, and he got fired. Seems like he's having a pretty shitty run. And not that we'd usually care, but we think the person who might have his fiancée is Cathy," River explains, sitting down on the daybed in my new office.

My jaw drops. "Okay, wow. I didn't see that one coming. Do you really think it's her?"

I've obviously heard about their grandmother and how she chose Victor over them all, and I know she pretty much got banished from the family, but I thought that was it, and she moved away and on with her life. I guess the old lady still has plenty of life and hate in her, which is sad. She'll probably only know peace when she dies.

"I don't know. All we know is that it's a woman, and she's the only one we can think of with a motive. Problem is we can't find her, and we really don't have much else to go on," he says, shrugging. "But Mark isn't going to try to put you in prison, especially after we let him go, so there is that."

"That is a good thing." I smirk, swiveling around on my chair to face him. "What do we do now?"

"Keep an eye out, don't trust anyone, the usual," he says. "I thought I could take you to go and visit my mom in the next few days. It's an hour's drive to get there."

"I'd like that." I smile, excitement filling me. "It might be nice to get away too, even if it's just a day trip."

And I love that he's letting me in. I know that being introduced to his mother is huge, and I'm not going to take it for granted.

"Good. Now I'm going to run some errands and I'll get you some lunch. What are you in the mood for?"

I give him my order for a pizza and after he leaves, I get some work done, making business calls. I'm going to have to go in to view some properties soon, but right now I'm not going to take on any new clients and leave my workload light. I'm lucky that money isn't an issue for me. I've always been a good saver and have a nice little nest egg in my account.

Corey is in the living room watching *Married at First Sight*, her arm around Hades while he snuggles in her lap, and I sit down and join her, getting pulled in quickly. "I should apply to go on this show," she says, laughing, which makes Hades jump. "Sorry, Hades," she says, rubbing his head, and turns back to me. "Could you imagine River sitting there and watching me? He'd be pissed."

"Yeah, I definitely wouldn't be watching it with him," I reply in a dry tone. "You don't need to go on a show like this—you'll have men throwing themselves at you when you are ready to date or settle down."

"Do you want to have kids?" she suddenly asks, looking at me. "Because I don't think I do, and I know that is going to deter a lot of men."

"I want kids, yes," I reply. "Two would be nice. And I'm sure there are men out there who don't want kids, or already have kids and are done having more."

"Maybe," she says, shrugging. "But I don't personally know any men who don't want children. Probably because they don't have to do as much work as we do to have them, and look after them."

"Depends on the man," I say, contemplating her words. "Obviously we do all the work at the beginning, but when the baby is born a good dad will help raise a child as much as a mother. I think Romeo will be a wonderful dad."

"So do I," she admits, hazel eyes gentling. "Maybe I'm a little cynical. My dad was an asshole."

"Sorry to hear that."

"Yeah, me, too. But at least he's not around anymore. How about you? You close with your parents?" she asks, resting her cheek on her palm.

"I think I was always like a third wheel with my parents. I'm an only child, and children didn't really fit into their lifestyle. They are very fun people, and they do love me. But I didn't have your stereotypical family growing up. I did a lot of things by myself."

"That's kind of sad," she blurts out.

"Yeah, I don't think about it much," I say, looking back to the TV. "But I'd definitely never have just one child. I look at you and River and feel a little let down that I didn't have that. I have Julianna, of course, and we are close, like sisters. And now I have you, too."

"Yeah." She smiles. "That's the best thing about our MC—we are just one big family. Everyone here is so nice and always willing to help. Like how cool is Jag? He only just got here, and he's already part of the family. And all the Angels MC, you guys are all cool. The younger crowd, anyway."

I laugh. "Yeah, I suppose the older members aren't fun anymore."

River shows up with pizza for everyone, and we all sit on the couch together and eat it. It's nice to just hang out. I try not to think about all the drama going on, but it's hard. Even though they let Mark go, he doesn't know that his car has a bug in it, and Jag got into his phone and security system while he was here. So if Mark betrays us, everyone will know, and we'll be able to determine if he was telling the truth about the whole thing or not. You never know with him—he's turned out to be quite the wild card. River tells me that even though things seem okay now, we need to be careful, because the danger isn't over.

And he's right.

We have to watch our backs and be on alert at all times.

The next day we go to meet River's mother, Lisa. I buy snacks for the drive, excited for our first mini road trip together. I made sure to dress nicely, in a long maxi dress and cute little cardigan, with natural makeup and my hair tied up. I really want Lisa to like me, and for her to know that her son is loved and taken care of.

"I love this song," I say, turning the volume up on "Life Goes On."

"You like to listen to sad songs, don't you?" he comments, amusement laced in his tone.

"I mean they make you feel, so yeah, I guess I do. I just love anything by Ed Sheeran, though. This album just happens to be a mostly sad one. What music do you like? You always listen to anything— I've never actually seen you put on a favorite band or something."

"Yeah, you're right, I kind of do just listen to anything," he replies, staring ahead at the road. "I like rap, metal, rock. Pretty much anything other than country."

"I don't mind country," I say, shrugging. "But noted. Do you like Ed?"

"If that's what you like and makes you happy, I'll listen to Ed all fucking day," he replies, reaching over to take my hand into his.

What a contradiction this man is.

The same hands that can be so violent can also be so sweet.

"Am I the first woman you've brought to meet your mom?" I ask, sighing in contentment as he runs his fingers up and down my thigh.

"Yes, you are. I haven't been in a committed relationship like this before. I never really wanted one, I don't think. But you kind of fell into my life, and now I can't imagine my life without you," he says, squeezing my thigh gently. "I was just waiting for the right person the whole time, apparently."

"What did you do before, just casually hook up?"

He nods. "Pretty much. Casual sex. Not as much as you're probably thinking. I wasn't a playboy like Romeo."

I laugh. "Well, that's a good thing. I'd have to find out that you've slept with any of my family members or friends." Like Romeo did with Rosalind before Julianna.

"No, I don't think you have to worry about that," he says.

I put on some nineties hits and the two of us sing along to them all until we arrive at a cute little town house right next to a forest near Mount Charleston.

River opens my door for me and helps me out,

and I grab the bouquet of flowers that I brought for his mom, not wanting to show up empty-handed.

And then we walk up to the front door and knock.

Chapter Twenty

River

Bella smiles at my mom and greets her warmly, giving her the flowers she brought. She doesn't react to her missing eye, and doesn't even seem to stare at the patch like I've seen other people do. I know I should have warned her, but I'm so used to it that it slipped my mind.

"It's so lovely to finally meet you," my mother says, beaming as she takes Bella in. "You are absolutely beautiful."

"Thank you, so are you. It's nice to meet you, too. Thank you for having me here," Bella says.

Mom ushers us inside and gets us seated, bringing out some snacks for us and offering to make us tea and coffee. "It's so nice to see River settle down with someone," she says, sighing happily as she looks between us. "So tell me about yourself, Bella."

"Um, well, I'm a property manager, and an only

child. I'm a Callisto, which I guess would have been a problem before, but isn't one anymore," she replies, smiling over at me. "I came as a package with my dog, Hades. How about yourself?"

"I grew up around the Devils MC, and raised my kids around them. But now I prefer my life of peace and solitude," Mom says. "I love it here—I foster animals and help run the local animal refuge. And there's no drama or violence. River comes around and helps me with anything I need; he's a good boy."

Bella looks over at me with warmth in her gaze. "Yes, he is."

We finish our coffee, and then Mom takes Bella for a tour while I chop up some more wood for her. From the back of the property, I can see them walking around and laughing, and see Mom introduce her to all the animals, which I know Bella will love.

Why didn't I bring her here sooner?

I know I was worried about her finding out about Robert, and she told me she wouldn't tolerate me lying to her again. If she asks what happened to Mom's eye, I'm going to have to tell her that my mother is a survivor of domestic violence. What I don't know if I'll tell her is what happened to Robert afterward. And I still haven't told anyone else about him not even being my biological father. But if she asks...

Bella walks over with a kitten in her hands. "Your mom is so nice, River. And she does so much for all the animals. I can see why she loves it out here."

She doesn't mention the eye, which I think is really nice of her.

"It is pretty great out here," I agree, patting the kitten on the head, and then giving Bella a kiss. We spend more time around the property, then head out for lunch before we drive home.

Mom gives Bella a big hug before we leave, and it's so nice to see them getting along like this. "Come back anytime," Mom says to her. "I'd love to see you both more. Thank you for coming."

Bella is happy the whole drive home, and I know it meant a lot to her to meet Mom. I feel like a fucking asshole for not doing it sooner.

We stop by her house to get a few things, then drive back to the clubhouse. My eyes narrow when I see Corey standing out the front, talking to Jag.

"They're friends," Bella says, smirking. "She was saying how he fits in here just like family. And he's a nice guy. Don't be an asshole to him. You can't hate every man who looks her way. She's a beautiful girl."

"I hope I don't have any daughters," I grumble. Because I'm clearly not cut out for letting them go.

"Do you want children? Corey asked me and then I realized that I didn't know how you felt about it," she asks.

I put the car in Park and turn to her, softening. "I thought I never wanted children, but to be honest with you, I could definitely see myself having a couple with you. I think you'd be a wonderful mother."

She smiles and leans over to kiss me. "I think you'd be a badass father. Changing diapers and all."

I smile and take her hand. Jag opens the door, interrupting our moment, and if looks could kill he would be dead on the floor.

"Thanks," she says to him, getting out.

"How was it?" Corey asks, a look of sadness flashing in her eyes. It must be so hard for her, and it's a shame both mother and daughter are too stubborn to reach out to each other first.

"It was lovely," Bella replies, linking arms with her. "Your mom has made a little paradise there for herself and animals that need her. Now what should we do for dinner?" Bella goes into the kitchen and begins searching through the fridge and freezer to see what we have.

"You going to cook again?" Corey asks, perking up.

"Yeah, maybe I'll go and get some steaks," Bella says, closing the fridge door. She grabs her bag and looks over at me. "Want to come to the store with me?"

"Yep," Corey says, looking over at me. "And we'll be fine, we don't need any extra babysitters."

Bella kisses me and heads out, so I go and join Jeremiah and Jag, who are watching Mark's home surveillance cameras.

"Anything?" I ask, pulling out a seat.

"He's made a few calls trying to find out where his Sarah is. We tried to listen to the voice on the line, but we could only tell it was female. This guy is kind of a mess. I wouldn't be surprised if he turned into an alcoholic or something," Jeremiah says, pointing to Mark sitting there downing a glass of vodka.

"I mean, his woman *is* being held hostage right now," Jag reminds him. "I also did some digging and found out why he got fired."

"Why?" I ask, curious.

"Well, apparently Sarah was another undercover job for him, and he wasn't supposed to be with her either, same as Bella. He went against the rules and told her the truth," he explains, wincing. "And now he's lost her and being blackmailed. It's pretty rough."

"I don't have the time to feel sorry for him," I say, pursing my lips. "We just need to figure out how to find the caller. I'm guessing the call was untraceable?"

Jag nods. "Burner phone."

"Maybe we just need to be there when she calls next, and speak to her ourselves? Where's Romeo?"

"Him and Julianna had some meeting to go to," Jeremiah says, looking back to the screen. "Where did the girls go?"

"They went to the store—Bella is going to cook us all dinner. If they aren't back in twenty minutes, I'll go look for them myself," I grumble.

Jag changes the screen, which shows the tracker he put in Bella's car. "There you go, you can watch them and see where they are going."

I laugh. Hard to admit it, but having Jag around

has been pretty good. Our setup wasn't as fancy as this prior to his arrival.

When I notice the car returning home, I head back outside so I can help them with the bags, checking out my bike while I'm waiting. Sometimes you just need some time to admire it. Once they are inside and cooking, I decide to go for a quick ride with Jeremiah.

With everything going on, sometimes it's nice to just take some time to yourself, clear your head and be thankful for what you have.

A ride is where I process things.

And it's about time that I face up to the things I've been ignoring.

My name is River Montanna, second son of Andrew and next in line to lead the Angels and Devils MC.

And I need to accept that.

Chapter Twenty-One

Bella

"Steaks, baked potatoes, corn on the cob, and a roasted beet and pumpkin salad," I announce, looking over at my spread. Julianna was going to cook tonight, but I offered and told her she could rest instead. I like looking after her when I can.

"If you don't marry her, I will," Jeremiah jokes, rubbing his hands together with glee and ignoring the death stare River sends his way.

"It looks incredible," River says, kissing my temple and then taking a seat. "We'd normally just order something in, so this is really nice. Thank you."

"You're welcome," I say, smiling as I watch them all dig in.

"Oh my God, the meat is so tender," Jag says, moaning. "Can you live here forever, please?"

"You don't even know if *you're* here forever,"

Corey says, laughing. "But yes, I agree. Never leave us, Bella."

We finish up the meal together, and I save some for Romeo and Julianna, who haven't returned, and then bring out dessert. "I made some brownies and bought some vanilla ice cream."

The way they look at me makes me laugh, like they've just seen the sun for the first time. We've all just finished dessert when we hear a loud bang, making me jump.

River is the first up, his eyes going to me. "You and Corey get in my bedroom and lock the door, now."

He runs to the front, along with the other men, and I grab Corey's arm and try to lead her away. But when we hear a gunshot, we both look at each other.

"What if one of them got shot?" she says, starting to freak out. "I'm not going to lose someone else I love and just stand around and do nothing. I can't go through that again!"

I try to hold on to her, but she pushes me off and runs to the front of the house.

"Corey!" I call, chasing after her. River is going to be pissed, but I can't let her go out there alone. When I step outside and look around, I'm shocked at what I see.

Mark is standing there pointing a gun at River.

Corey has been shoved behind Jag to protect her, and Jeremiah is on the ground, shot in the arm. River's eyes widen in fear when he sees me out in the open.

"What are you doing, Mark?" I ask, trying to ignore the fact that my ex-boyfriend is pointing a gun at the man I love. "Come on, this isn't you. And we haven't done anything to you."

Besides beat him and hold him hostage.

"She said she will return Sarah if I kill Romeo. Where is he? I'm sorry, but I'll do anything to get her back. I don't want to hurt you, Bella. Just go back inside," he calls out, returning his gaze to River. "Call Romeo, now, and tell him to come back to the clubhouse."

He has officially lost his mind.

River gets his phone out of his jeans pockets and dials Romeo. I can't hear what he says, but I'm sure he somehow gives Romeo a heads-up that shit isn't great here right now. Julianna does not need to come here; if she gets hurt while pregnant, I'll never forgive myself. I slowly move over to Jeremiah and take off my cardigan, wrapping it around his arm to help stop the bleeding.

"You okay?" I ask quietly.

He nods. "Yeah, I'm fine. Or at least I will be. We need to take this guy out."

"Why don't you let the women and Jeremiah go inside? He needs medical attention. I'll wait with you until Romeo gets here," River suggests to Mark, staying calm and collected.

Mark considers it, looking over at me and Jeremiah, then nods. "The women can go inside. Everyone else wait out here."

River looks at me. "Bella, take Corey and go inside."

I nod, wanting to call Julianna to make sure she doesn't come here. "Corey, come on."

She doesn't move, so I grab her arm and pull her back inside. "We need to warn Julianna," I tell her, getting my phone off the table and calling her number. Corey goes to her bedroom. Julianna doesn't pick up, so I send her a text.

Bella: Do not come to the clubhouse. Mark is here with a gun. He wants Romeo dead.

When Corey comes back out with a gun in her hands, my eyes widen in shock. "Ah, Corey! What are you doing? Do you know how to use that thing?"

She nods. "I was raised a Devil. I don't know what they did with you Angels, but here women were taught how to use a gun. I know exactly what I'm doing. If I had a sniper rifle, I could probably take him out without having to go there. But all I have is my nine-millimeter Glock."

Wait, what?

I look at the gun in her hands, which just looks like a handgun to me. "Corey, don't do anything stupid. River will never forgive me if something happens to you."

And I will never forgive her if something happens to him.

My phone beeps with a text from Julianna.

Julianna: I'm safe at Grandma's. Romeo is going there with some men. Coming up from the back. You guys stay inside.

"Corey, we need to stay inside—Julianna just texted, look." I show her the message, and she stops in her tracks.
"Okay, okay, I'll wait," she agrees.
Thank goodness.

Bella: I'm inside with Corey. Men are out front. Mark is alone and pointing a gun at River. Jeremiah is shot but just a flesh wound.

Julianna: Hide in your room just in case. Stay safe.

I grab Corey and do as we're told. I just need to hope that Romeo comes in time, and that nothing happens to River.

When we hear another gunshot, we both share a look. Now I'm jealous that I don't know how to use a goddamn gun. It'd be pretty useful right about now.

I don't want to see Mark dead, but if someone has to go down, I'd rather it be him.

Chapter Twenty-Two

River

With the women safely out of the way, I feel comfortable taking some risks. I'm not waiting for Romeo.

I wait until the most opportune moment, when Mark's focusing on Jeremiah, probably wondering if he's going to bleed out, and run for him, knocking the gun out of his hands. It goes off, but hits one of our cars instead of anyone else. Jag runs over and gets the gun, and I roll Mark over and pin his hands behind his back. He struggles, bucking his legs and trying to free his arms, but I hold steady. Good luck if he thinks he's going to overpower me.

Romeo arrives shortly after with a few of the older men and Damon.

"What are we going to do with him?" I ask.

"I have no fucking idea," he replies gruffly, heading into the house with him. Looks like it's back into the garage for our old friend Mark.

I rush inside to check on Bella, and find her and Corey in the kitchen pouring everyone alcohol. Even though they are supposed to be in the bedroom, I can see the appeal. Much needed. She runs up for a hug as soon as she sees me. "Thank God you are okay."

"Take a lot more than that dumbass to take me down," I say, kissing the top of her head.

Corey hugs me from the side, wrapping her arm around Bella, too. "Do you want a drink?"

"I'd love one," I say, before swallowing a shot of tequila in one gulp.

Damon steps into the kitchen. "You ladies okay?"

"Yeah, we're good," Bella replies.

"Tequila?" Corey offers, holding out another shot glass. Damon grins and reaches out to accept.

Bella takes a shot herself, slams the empty glass down, then pulls me out of the room. "What's going to happen now?"

"I don't know," I admit, holding her against me. "Mark was obviously desperate to save his woman, and I can't blame him for that. I don't think any of us can. But we can't exactly just let him free to try to kill our president again. Jag took Jeremiah to the hospital to be checked on. We have a doctor we're friends with there who won't ask any questions, but we're lucky it didn't kill him. Mark's obviously not in the right headspace right now."

Understatement. The man is a loose cannon, and he needs to be contained before he does something stupid. That, or simply put out of his misery.

I know which one I'd vote for.

I don't like leaving Corey alone with Damon, but I'm trying not to be too unreasonably overprotective of her. And when Bella tells me how she came out with her gun, wanting to join in on the fight, I need to remember that although she is hurting, she is still the badass sister I helped raised.

Albeit a little fucking impulsive.

No idea where she got that from.

As if there wasn't enough drama for one day, the police show up and ask us if we've seen Mark. I'm pretty sure they are his cop friends and not here on official business, because they don't arrest anyone or give us any trouble. Which is probably the first time that has ever happened. Romeo looks over at me, the two of us contemplating what we should do, while the cops stand at the door waiting. Do we hand him over? It would buy us time to keep him away from us, but also he is our only lead to our grandma, because she contacts him and no one else.

Although I suppose we only need his phone, not him.

When I open the garage, he's sitting on a chair with his head down on the desk. "Mark, come on. There's some people here to see you."

"What people?" he asks, blinking furiously. "The FBI?"

"Yeah, sure," I mutter, helping him up.

Romeo grabs him and delivers him to the police out front, explaining how Mark showed up with a gun, and we have video surveillance to prove that. These cops look like they don't care what the hell we were doing with him, they just want him, for what I have no idea. Probably something shady, because that seems to be Mark's trademark.

We send him on his merry way, handing over his gun to the cops, then lock up and hide in the clubhouse, not wanting to deal with any more shit today. Jag returns with a patched-up Jeremiah, who we sit on the couch with movies and beer. "You took Mark's phone when he got here, right?

"I know we can't trace the calls, but maybe we can try to speak to her," I suggest to Romeo, who is about to leave to get Julianna.

"Yeah, that will have to be a me job," he replies, rubbing the back of his neck in frustration. "I don't know if it's safer to leave Julianna with her family or bring her back here, but she wants to be here. And I'd rather be with her."

"Yeah, she's safest with us all," I agree, resting my hand on his shoulder. "You know we would all do anything to protect her."

"I know."

He goes to pick her up and I find Bella in the gym walking on the treadmill. She removes her headphones when she sees me.

"Will you show me how to shoot a gun?" she asks, surprising me. "Just in case, I want to be able to defend myself."

"Yes, I can show you," I say.

She smiles and puts her headphones back on, so I decide to join her and lift some weights and punch our boxing bag.

It's been a weird week, and there's still some things I haven't dealt with, but we're all still here and healthy and together, so I can't really complain about anything.

An hour later, we finish up our workout and are walking to our bedroom to have a shower, when we come across Corey in the hallway.

Kissing Damon.

I really fucking try to not lose control, but all I can see is red.

Chapter Twenty-Three

Bella

I warned Damon not to mess with Corey, but he didn't listen.

When River sees them, he pulls Damon off her by his T-shirt and then punches him in the face. It doesn't stop there—Damon fights him back but River just keeps going for him. Corey tries to stop it, but I don't want her to get accidentally hit, so I pull her away and call for the men. Jeremiah and Jag rush over and get between them and stop it, but Damon walks away with his face covered in blood.

It looks bad.

Damon is a good fighter, but River was in a rage, and he wasn't holding back.

Corey starts crying, and I do feel bad for her, but she was playing with fire and she knew that. She should at least not do it right in front of everyone. But River was out of line to get so aggressive, and I know he must feel bad now. Not that he'd ever admit it. And if he doesn't, he should.

He comes out of the shower, knuckles busted, and a cut lip from a hit that Damon got in. I have to give it to him, Damon didn't go down without a fight. But there's too much going on right now and we don't need the men in our own MC at war, too. We need to be one, a unit, and not carrying on like this.

"Corey is an adult," I say gently. "She's a woman, not just your little sister."

"I know," he replies, sitting down on the bed in his towel. "But she's young and inexperienced."

"And why do you think she's inexperienced?" I ask in a dry tone, blinking quickly. "She's never had a chance to casually date, or do anything the rest of us did, because you scare the shit out of anyone interested in her!"

A muscle works in his jaw. "She's not in the right place to date someone."

"Even if that's true, it's her decision. It's her life," I say, moving closer to him and resting my head on his shoulder. "I love you, River. More than anything. But I'm telling you, she is going to pull away from you if you can't treat her like an adult."

"That's my baby sister, and I don't want her with a guy like that," he says, gritting his teeth.

"A guy like what?" I ask, brow furrowing. "Damon is a nice person, and trust me, she could do a lot worse."

A muscle works in his jaw. "Look, I shouldn't

have reacted the way I did, but I still don't like it. I will apologize to her."

"I think that's a great idea."

I've never been so happy to be an only child in my life.

Corey is sitting outside in the dark looking at the stars when I go looking for her. I turn the light on and join her.

"Damon went home?" I gather.

She nods. "Yeah, I cleaned him up and gave him an ice pack for his face. Then Romeo came back and was pissed, told Damon to go."

I imagine he would be angry; he left the clubhouse for twenty minutes and came back to that. He's already stressed enough with all that has been happening and with Julianna being pregnant.

"I'm sorry, Corey. That shouldn't have turned into such a big...thing," I mutter, reaching out and holding her hand.

"It was my fault. I'm the one who kissed him," she says, looking over at me with tears in her eyes. "I should have been more private, I know. I was an idiot, but I just got lost in the moment."

"It will be okay," I promise her. "And don't feel bad, it wasn't your fault. I did warn Damon, so he knew what he was getting into."

"Why am I stuck with the brother who has to be warned about?" she grumbles, scrubbing her hands down her face. "I love him, but oh my god, he can be so frustrating. It was just a kiss. My first kiss, actually, and not one I'll be forgetting anytime soon."

Her first kiss?

Fucking hell.

"Oh, Corey," I sigh, really feeling for her.

The sliding door opens and a freshly dressed River steps outside, his hair damp. I stand up to leave, but Corey says, "No, don't go."

River sits on the other side of her. "I'm sorry, I shouldn't have reacted like that. It just took me by surprise to see you…kissing someone. I'm your older brother and it's my job to look after you. And I know how men think and I just…want you with someone good."

"How do you know who is good if you aren't going to give anyone a chance?" she asks, looking over at him. "I'm not a child anymore, and I need to be able to have a little freedom without worrying about you coming in with guns blazing."

"I mean, could you not have your freedom in the clubhouse hallway?" he asks, clearing his throat.

She laughs a little. "Yeah, I guess that sounds fair."

He holds his arms out and they hug, and it's very sweet. And then she reaches over to me and gives me a hug, too. "Thank you," she says, smiling.

I don't think I did anything, but I smile in return, just happy that she's no longer upset and the two of them are on good terms again.

We do not need any more drama for a long time.

"There's something I need to tell you," River says when we get back to our room.

"What is it?" I ask, sitting cross-legged on the bed.

He starts to pace, and that's how I know that this is something important. "Remember the night we had the party here for Jeremiah's birthday?"

"Yeah."

"Romeo's mom was drunk, and she told me something. She said that my father was really Andrew, Romeo's dad, not Robert, who I always thought was my father," he says, stopping and pinning me with sad, blue eyes. "I asked my mom and she admitted it was true. I don't know if Andrew knows or not, but…"

I stand up and hug him tightly. "You've just been holding on to that?"

"Yeah, I think I just needed to process it before I told you," he says, rubbing my back with his big hands. "It just took me off guard. Robert was an asshole. He was abusive. You saw my mother's eye? That was because of him. He was an angry and violent man, and he didn't make our childhood easy. And to find out now that the whole time he wasn't even my biological father?"

Shit. It's a lot to process. "Do I want to ask you what happened to Robert?"

He freezes and holds my gaze. "Do you want to ask what happened to him?"

"Do you remember what I said to you when I saw

you in the garage?" I know this is a turning point in our relationship.

"I do. So I want you to know that I will tell you the truth if you ask me. But we can't walk it back once I do. Is this really what you want?"

His words give me pause. He's going to tell me the truth. He's going to answer me. Shit. I really think about what this would do to him and what he is saying.

I take a breath. "Let's say I don't ask. But assume I know. Do you think what I am assuming is correct?" I'm assuming Robert will never see the light of day.

He clenches his jaw. "It frustrates me that I know what you're assuming. But what you are assuming is most likely true."

I nod and put a hand on his forearm. "Thank you for being as honest as you can be with me. I love you."

He nods his head and looks down. I know I need to change the subject. "You haven't told Romeo? About Andrew?"

He shakes his head. "No, I don't think I've been ready to speak about it until now. I know I should have told you earlier, and I'm sorry I didn't. I just needed a little time before I said it out loud. And as for Romeo, I will talk to him. I don't know how he's going to take it."

"I wish you did tell me sooner, but I understand it must have been hard for you to process. You've been like brothers with Romeo this whole time—this will just make it official," I say, kissing him gently. "And I'm here for you no matter what. You know this."

He rests his forehead against mine and closes his eyes. "It's us against the world."

Us and the whole MC against the world.

Chapter Twenty-Four

River

I feel lighter after telling Bella about what Aunty Victoria told me. And I know that I can trust her and that is fucking huge for me, because I usually don't trust anyone.

Next up I have to tell Romeo. I know the timing isn't the best because his stress levels are already extremely high, but waiting for the right moment will take forever.

There's no right moment for this.

"Did you know that was Corey's first kiss today?" Bella asks me before I leave the room to find Romeo, making me feel like utter shit.

That was her first kiss?

At nineteen years old.

I never would have guessed that. I know I'm over-protective, but I'm not always around and I never thought she'd be waiting for a kiss at her age.

Shit.

She's a good girl, and I've messed up big-time.

I don't feel bad for Damon, though—that asshole should have known better, coming into my clubhouse and kissing my sister.

Yeah, I don't fucking think so.

Instead of finding Romeo, I stumble across Julianna sitting in the kitchen alone eating ice cream. With pickles.

"I think you're taking this a little too far," I say, pulling out a chair and sitting next to her.

"Blame the baby, not me," she replies, grinning. "So, today was crazy."

"Which part of the day are you referring to?" I ask in a dry tone.

She gets an extra bowl and spoon and scoops some ice cream for me, minus the pickles, which I appreciate.

"Thank you," I say as she slides me the bowl.

"Well, I mean, you couldn't really control the Mark thing, but the Damon thing…"

"Don't you start," I say quietly, eating the cookies and cream in front of me. "I've already had to speak to Corey and Bella about this, we made up, I'm done with it."

"Okay," she replies, dragging out the word.

"Where's Romeo?"

"He was having a shower when I left," she says, tucking her blonde hair back behind her pierced ears. "Is everything okay?"

"Yeah, just wanted to chat with him before I went to bed, but it's okay." I scoop the last bit from the bowl and put it in the sink just as Jag runs into the kitchen, Mark's phone in his hand.

"The kidnapper finally called, so I answered and said Romeo would like to speak with her, but she hung up. I recorded the voice so maybe you might recognize it," he says, playing back the woman's slightly distorted voice saying, *"Mark? I let Sarah go, now keep your end of the deal."*

We can then hear Jag speaking to her, and then her hanging up. I know this voice, I just can't place it. However, it doesn't sound like Cathy, which is concerning, because who the hell are we dealing with here?

"Play it for Romeo," I suggest, just as he steps into the kitchen.

"We having a meeting or something?" he asks, smirking as he sees Julianna dipping pickles into her bowl.

"Play it," I tell Jag. He plays it again for us to hear.

"That's not Grandma's voice," Romeo says after listening to it for a few times. "I don't think so, anyway. It's a younger voice."

"Wait, play it again," Julianna says, frowning. "It sounds familiar."

No one can place it, so we call it a night and head to bed. I don't get to speak with Romeo, but I tell myself that I'll talk to him tomorrow.

At least Mark got his damn Sarah back, so hopefully he won't show up here again, because if he does, we're going to have to kill him.

I'm done playing games with him.

The next morning I take Bella to the shooting range. She's right—knowing how to shoot is a very good thing. That along with some self-defense can never go astray. I show her how to hold the gun and teach her all about gun safety.

She points at the target and misses on her first try.

But the second one?

Almost a bull's-eye.

"You're a good shot," I tell her, smiling.

I show off a little and demonstrate how it's done, hitting the target almost perfectly with every shot I fire.

"Okay, I want to be that good," she says, a determined expression on her beautiful face. "I didn't think I'd enjoy it, but it's kind of fun."

After two hours there I take her to a local Muay Thai gym to learn some moves from a famous fighter named Titan. I realize it wasn't the best idea when I have to watch this badass fighter man with his hands all over my woman, but it's educational.

At least that's what I keep telling myself.

When he has her on the ground teaching her how to get out of a hold, I consider fighting him even though I'm going to get my ass kicked, considering he's a world champion. Next time I'm just going to teach her my damn self. I know how to fight. Why the hell did I think bringing her here was a good idea?

I practice self-control and being the new me I've been promising everyone, and remind myself that she's mine and she's not going anywhere.

I have no reason to be jealous. She's coming home with me.

I'm not going to lie, though, I exhale in relief when the session is over, and she looks over at me with a wide smile.

See, I can control myself.

I am not Robert's son. And it doesn't matter who my father is anyway.

Because I am my own man.

I control who I am, what I do and how I react to things.

I am who I choose to be.

"Today was so fun," she says before putting her helmet on to ride home. "Thanks for taking me, River. I did things I've always wanted to do, and got out of my comfort zone. And I really enjoyed myself."

She gives me a kiss and a smile, and then jumps on the back of my bike.

And yeah, it was all worth it.

I guess that's what love is.

Chapter Twenty-Five

Bella

Do you ever wake up in the morning and you just
forget where you are? And who you are? I woke up
like that, still half lost in the weird dream I was having, half in the real world, and feeling confused. In
the dream I was running for my life, trying to get to
River in time, and someone was after me. I'm glad
to have woken from it.

Rolling over, I see River still fast asleep, so I snug-
gle up against him, spooning him from behind. I'm
glad he told me about Andrew being his father. I feel
sad his family kept that from him until now, and let
him think another man was his dad. Another man
who wasn't a good role model in any way, shape or
form, it sounds like. I had wondered what happened
to his mother's eye, but I didn't want to ask; I figured he'd tell me when he was ready, and he did. It
hurts me to think about the life she must have led,

and I can see why she wants to hide out away from everyone she knew.

And River.

He has so much on his shoulders. He's obviously always been the protector in the family, for his mother and his siblings, and now for an entire motorcycle club. And he doesn't know where that line is, and when to turn that off.

He's probably living in fight-or-flight mode, except for him he only goes into fight.

Fight-or-fight mode.

Pressing my cheek against his back, I hold him tight, wanting to protect him for once. I don't know if Andrew knew River was his son, but if he did and decided to just let him be around a violent man, then he is an asshole. Although I suppose he sent his own kid there to be raised by Lisa too, so I can't really put it past him. River's had a hard life, but he's a good man. Yes, he has his demons, but who doesn't?

I let him sleep in, and quietly leave the room to get some breakfast. Hades jumps off the couch to greet me, and I give him a pat before frying some bacon, sausage and eggs to eat with toast. After I give Hades a sausage, Julianna is the first to come out of bed, her pregnant nose leading her straight to the food.

"That smells so good, it woke me up," she says, grabbing a plate. "You are the best, you know that?"

She adds a side of pickles to hers, smiling up at me as she does so.

The men all follow in afterward, including a freshly showered River, who picks me up and lifts me in the air to spin me around, before kissing me as he puts me back on the ground. "You feeding everyone again?"

"Yes," I laugh. And I like it. I'm a nurturer, what can I say. Everyone eating what I've made makes me happy.

"Where's Corey?" Romeo asks, when she doesn't come out to eat.

"I'll go check on her," I say, walking to her room and knocking on her door, quiet at first but then louder. I open it when there's no answer, to find her bed empty. Shit. Did she sneak out? Is she okay?

Wincing that I'm going to have to tell River this news, I go back into the kitchen. "Okay, River, don't freak out, but she's not in bed. She must have gotten up early and gone somewhere."

River pulls out his phone to call her, putting her on speaker. She picks up right away. "Yeah?"

"Where are you?" he asks, fingers gripping his phone tightly.

"I'm on my way to visit Mom. I think it's time I see her, especially since she finally reached out to me," she says. "I'll be back this evening."

"Okay," he replies, exhaling in relief. "Drive safe."

Everyone seems to accept that explanation, but something about it doesn't sit right with me. Would she up and leave last minute without mentioning anything? I send her a text.

Bella: You okay? Just checking in.

"Do you think it's weird that Corey just left without saying anything, or is that normal for her?" I ask River as I undress to get into the shower.

"It's not unusual for her, but I am surprised that she'd go see my mom. It's a good thing, though—they need to work on their relationship. I'm glad that Corey is being the bigger person and making amends," he says, leaving the bathroom.

I think it's a good thing too, but it should be the parent who reaches out to fix the relationship, shouldn't it? That's how I think of it. With any future children that I have, it would be up to me to maintain a good, healthy relationship with them.

I guess every family dynamic is different, though, and I hope they can both be happier with each other back in their lives.

After getting dressed, I tidy up the bedroom and office, and then sit down to check my emails when I get a text. Panic feels me as I read it.

Corey: Help!

Bella: Where are you??

I yell out for River, and run to the front of the clubhouse, where the men are fixing their bikes.

"What is it?" he asks, and I show him the message.

"I knew something was wrong—I don't know, I just felt it," I say, panicking when I think about something bad happening to her.

"Bella, calm down," Romeo says, and then starts barking orders. "Jag, go and track her car and see where she is. Everyone else get armed and meet back here in five minutes. We are going after her. Jeremiah, call the Angels clubhouse and tell them to send some men over to stay with the women. And whoever touches a hair on her head is going to fucking pay for it."

"Yes, they will," River growls, taking my hand and leading me back indoors. "Stay inside. I'll give you a gun in case, but don't use it unless you really fucking have to."

Jag comes out of his room with information. "Her car's sitting on the side of the road. We can go straight to it and look for clues."

"Wait, is there a tracker in my car?" I ask, arching my brow. I'm met with silence, but I already know the answer.

"I'll take that as a yes. I'm texting Damon," I say. "He needs to know."

Bella: Corey is missing. Her car is on the side of the road.

Damon: I'm coming there now.

River kisses me deeply, then rushes out to save his baby sister. The one I told him he didn't need to protect.

What a fucking mess.

Chapter Twenty-Six

River

Even though I'm trying to stay calm and collected, inside I'm dying. Nothing can happen to my sister— I will never forgive myself.

Damon arrives, and I don't miss the panic in his eyes. I know exactly how he feels, and I don't have the time to argue with him now. The tightness of his jaw lets us know he's not going to take no for an answer, and I don't think even Romeo could stop him.

"We need someone to stay behind," I say, giving him a long look.

Testing him?

Maybe.

He throws a glance in my direction. "Well, it's not fucking going to be me."

I take a step in his direction.

"I can wait," Jag offers, looking between me and Damon, stopping me in my tracks. "I'll probably be more help from the security room anyway."

"Okay," Romeo agrees, nodding. I don't miss the assessing stare he gives Damon. "Damon, you listen to whatever I say. We need everyone to stay focused. Do you understand?"

Damon nods, rolling his shoulders back. "Yes, I'll do whatever I have to."

Right answer.

"I'll send you the coordinates for her car," Jag says, nodding. "Good luck."

"Look after them," I say, and he puts his hand on his heart.

"You know I will."

He goes inside and I get on my Harley, ready to go and bring Corey home where she belongs. And whoever has her? They have fucked with the wrong man.

The rumble of engines fires up and then we are off, following behind Romeo, darting by other cars on the road, until we see Corey's on the side of a main road. We all stop to inspect it. Nothing looks too amiss, except the keys are still in the engine and there's a burner phone on the front seat.

I pick it up, my fingers trembling slightly and hand it to Romeo, while I keep looking for anything else that might help us. It rings a few moments later.

Romeo has a short conversation with them, and then ends the call.

"What did they say?" I ask, gritting my teeth.

If anything happens to my sister—

"They gave me an address to go to, but only I

can show up or they will kill her," he says, clenching his jaw.

Fuck.

"You're not going alone," I reply. If he does, they will kill him. He'd be giving them what they want and walking right into their trap. And if he goes in alone, Corey might not make it out if it goes to hell and no one else is there to save her.

"We can stay close by," Jeremiah suggests, scanning the area. "What other options do we have?"

"They'll hear the bikes—we need a car," Damon says, eying Corey's. "What are the chances that they've done something to this one?"

"It's on a main road. I don't think they would have time to do anything other than grab her," I say, watching the many cars drive past.

Romeo paces a little, hands in his hair in frustration. "Okay, I'll go on my bike, the rest of you take the car. I'll call Jag and tell him the location and see if he can tell us the best way to do this."

We don't have a fucking plan.

We just need to show up, and hope for the best, because there is no alternative.

Corey is going to get out of there alive, or I'm going to set this fucking town on fire.

And judging by the hard look on Damon's face, he's going to help me.

I get in the driver's seat and wait for Romeo to make up the plan with Jag. Jeremiah and Damon get in the car. Damon still looks like shit, with a black eye and swollen face, and if I wasn't such an asshole I'd probably apologize to him for that.

Romeo shows me a map on his phone. "They want me to go to this warehouse. You guys could park right here. Just know that they are likely expecting this, and I have no idea what we're walking into right now."

"We will make it work, we always do," I tell him, nodding. "Let's go, we've got this."

Except we fucking don't. We're going in blind. We don't even know how many people will be there, nothing.

But fuck it, I've had a good run.

As long as we get Corey out safely, I don't fucking care what happens to me.

I put the location into my GPS and get on our way.

"I hope we fucking know what we are doing," Jeremiah says. He's wearing his usual leather getup; I just hope he can run in those pants.

"We just need to get her out alive. I don't care what we need to do," Damon says, echoing my thoughts from the back seat. I hate to admit it, but I'm glad he's here. I need someone with that mentality. Because I don't care what we need to fucking do either.

There's no boundaries I wouldn't cross right now to make sure she gets home safe and sound.

We drive behind Romeo, then part as we get closer to the warehouse. We go around the back and park, while Romeo heads up the front and gets off his bike.

As he walks in with his hands in the air, we move closer on foot, surrounding the warehouse exits.

Do they have her standing out there with them, waiting for Romeo? I wonder if I can run in when the time's right, guns blazing, and—

I freeze when I feel the barrel of cold steel pushed against my temple. I curse myself for being so distracted and not seeing that coming.

Concentrate, River.

"Get up," a familiar voice says. I stand up and turn around to look at Mark. That piece of shit. "I knew you'd show up."

I want to murder him with my bare hands, but I need him to walk me inside the warehouse so I can see what's going on and figure out how to get us all out.

"You're the one who took Corey?" I ask.

He shakes his head. "No, I'm not. Come on."

When I step inside the warehouse, I see Romeo sitting on a chair, and in front of him is none other than Cathy.

Now that isn't a surprise to me, at all. We had a suspicion it was her trying to kill Romeo in revenge for him killing Victor.

But the real shock is the person standing next to Cathy.

Rosalind.

Julianna's sister, and Romeo's ex.

Hell hath no fury like a woman scorned.

This bitch must have been holding on to this anger

and decided to team up with Cathy to get some old-fashioned revenge. She played it well, because we thought she was cool with Julianna, and that all was forgiven.

We welcomed her into our home.

"We knew that wherever Romeo is, you would be," Cathy says, pursing her pink lips. "I was only going to kill Romeo, but I suppose taking out his enforcer is also a win."

"I thought you and Julianna were close now," Romeo says to Rosalind, his jaw clenched tight.

She tilts her head back and laughs. "That's what I wanted you to think. Did you think I was going to let you get away with what you did to me? You broke my heart, and then gave yours to my sister. You killed Victor, who Veronica loved, and then you took over our MC. You've done damage to everyone with your selfishness, Romeo. It's about time you learned a lesson. Cathy told me that I'm allowed to be angry. My feelings matter, too. It's not just about Julianna."

"It was you on the phone," I say, realizing the truth. "You were calling Mark and threatening him, not Cathy."

Rosalind smirks and looks over at Mark. "Yes, it was me. We put a hit out on Romeo, but after the first man went missing, no one wanted to do the job. Then sweet Bella became the perfect target. After a little digging, Cathy found out that Mark was with the FBI, and I knew he would help me."

Roger went into hiding, and looks like he did a good job of it.

"The forged signature," I say, giving Rosalind a bit of credit for the smart plan.

Rosalind smiles, an evil glint in her eyes. "Wasn't that just perfect? Dear Sally also was a plant. I promised her a load of money if she could keep me posted on what was going on with Julianna and Bella. When she gave me the perfect opportunity to get dirt on Bella? I took it. Bella practically gave me a gift—it was too perfect. So all I had to do was let the information casually fall in Mark's lap. And then there was Sarah..."

"What about Sarah?" I ask, confused.

"I am Sarah," Rosalind laughs, winking at Mark, who keeps his expression blank. "We're in love and would do anything for each other. He was investigating me, or at least my alias. He lost his job at the FBI because of me. And when he thought I was kidnapped, he did whatever was asked of him to get me back. He has proved his loyalty to me, tenfold. I sent my friends dressed up as cops to pick him up from your clubhouse that day, and you guys didn't even bat an eyelash." She laughs again, but there's no emotion behind her eyes. "They weren't even real cops! I can't believe the shit you've let happen. You have all lost control, and I've been loving every second of it. Combining clubs has been the stupidest move you've ever made."

Shit. So she has been using Mark like a puppet

this whole time, playing with his emotions by letting him think she was in danger, and he's still sticking by her? What the fuck is wrong with him? I know her pussy can't be that good, otherwise Romeo would have hung around longer.

Cathy looks over her firstborn grandson. "It's sad it has come to this, Romeo. But I lost everything because of you. I got exiled from the family. And now they are all going to feel the pain that I felt."

"Grandma—"

She looks over at me and smiles. "I heard that you finally learned the truth. It was Victoria, wasn't it? Give that woman alcohol and her lips are looser than her legs. I've always known, from the day that you were born."

Romeo glances over at me with confusion in his eyes, and I suppose I have some explaining to do. But now is not the time, which Cathy is more than aware of. She just likes to cause trouble everywhere she goes. I must admit, though, I never saw this team-up happening. Apparently Callistos and Montannas can get along—when they both have a mutual enemy.

I look up and see Jeremiah and Damon slowly enter through the other exit, fluid and graceful, and then it's on. I'm so done listening to these two.

I spin and knock Mark out in one quick movement, just like I did at home in the clubhouse, then I pull out my gun and aim it at his head. His eyes widen as he falls back onto the ground, still facing me, and his mouth opens to object. But it's too late.

He had his chance to make the right choice, and he didn't. I pull the trigger and shoot him in the head, taking him out in one lethal shot. Him being Bella's ex just makes it even easier.

I said I'm done playing and I fucking mean it.

Rosalind screams, and I wince from the piercing sound. She tries to run to Mark, but Damon grabs her with an arm around her shoulders and holds her back. Jeremiah unties Romeo, struggling a bit with his injured hand. When Romeo is free, he walks right up to Grandma Cathy and looks her in the eyes.

"You're not going to stop, are you?" he asks her.

She shakes her head. "No. I have nothing to lose, Romeo."

And that makes her a very dangerous person.

Only our grandma would be a fucking villain instead of baking cookies.

"Where is Corey?" I ask them, steel in my tone. I probably should have asked before I killed Rosalind's lover, but them kidnapping my sister has made me a little trigger-happy. And if Corey isn't safe, it won't end with just Mark.

"Why would I tell you?" Rosalind cries, trying to get out of Damon's hold. "You killed him! What, are you jealous that I've moved on now?"

Holy fuck, she is crazy.

"Where is Corey?" Romeo demands of Cathy, whose eyes flicker, but she stays silent. She knows Romeo wouldn't hurt her. She's a woman, and older, and our fucking grandma.

"Corey is fine!" Rosalind eventually screams, tears dripping down her cheeks.

Jeremiah, who has been searching around the warehouse, eventually finds her in the trunk of their car, tied up with duct tape. He removes the tape from her mouth and lifts her out.

"Took you long enough," she calls out when she sees me, but her voice is shaky, and I know she must be rattled. She then turns and sees Damon there, and her eyes widen in surprise. Jeremiah holds her up while he unties her wrists, strain etched across his face.

After a few moments, she walks right up to Rosalind, looks her right in the eyes and then slaps her across her face. The sound echoes throughout the warehouse, and no one moves as we watch them intently. "I saw her on the side of the road, so I stopped to help her. That's how they got me. I stopped to fucking help you, Rosalind. You are the worst type of woman and you are nothing like your sister at all. I don't even know how the two of you are related. Romeo was right to leave your evil, spoiled ass." She looks to Mark, dead on the ground. "I feel bad for him, but you got what you deserved."

Rosalind cups her cheek with her hand, tears still dripping down her cheeks. "Corey—"

"Don't fucking speak to me ever again!"

Damon holds Corey's hand and scans her face to make sure she's okay, and I look away, feeling like I'm intruding on a private moment.

We decide to take the women back to the club-house. I don't think either of us are capable of killing our own grandmother.

And as for Rosalind?

She's going to be her father's problem.

Chapter Twenty-Seven

Bella

After a few hours, the men come back with Corey safe and well, and I cry in happiness. She runs into my arms when she sees me, and I hold her closely.

"Were you really on the way to your mom's?" I ask her.

She nods, her hazel eyes filled with sadness. "I was, but only because I got a message from my mom asking me to. Except it wasn't her at all—it was them."

I hug her harder, my heart breaking for her. "I'm just glad that you are home safely. Now can you never leave the clubhouse again, please?"

She laughs and wipes away some tears. "I don't want to upset Julianna while she's pregnant, but her sister was behind this with Cathy. I don't know what they are going to do with her."

River gave me a quick rundown when he first came in, and I can't imagine how Julianna is feeling right now. Rosalind used to go out for lunches with Juli-anna, or sometimes come here for dinner and hang out with us all, which was probably her getting in-formation to use to her advantage. It's why she knew that there was a rift between Corey and her mother. Julianna truly is the rose that came from concrete with her family. She is the only one with true integ-rity and loyalty.

And Sally? Sally was paid off by Rosalind and set me up. Well, again. That was me. I'm the one who gave Rosalind a tiny in. I allowed her plan to go into action.

"You don't worry about that," I tell Corey, push-ing hair off her face. "They will figure it all out. Do you want me to run you a bath or something so you can relax?"

She nods. "That sounds great. Did you see where Damon went? I saw him at the warehouse and then he went missing."

"I think he left," I say, walking with her to her bathroom. "But I know that he was determined to go and make sure that you were safe. He obviously cares about you. He was still rushing to protect you even with his black eye."

She grins and sighs dramatically. "I didn't expect to see him there. I knew River would be…"

"Okay, you better stop smiling now," I tease, sit-ting by the tub and turning the water on and check-ing the temperature. I put the plug in and add some Epsom salts. "I hope now we can get some peace around here, because I don't think I can take much more."

"Tell me about it," she groans, tying her red hair in a knot on top of her head. "I've never been in the trunk of a car before, but it was scary. Especially with the tape covering my mouth; it felt like I couldn't breathe. I felt so claustrophobic." She pauses. "Did River tell you about Mark?"

I pause and shake my head. "No, what about him?"

She cringes, then tries to backtrack. "Uh, never mind."

"Corey, tell me," I demand.

"He was there," she explains, shifting on her feet. "He was with them. He was in love with Rosalind, but he knew her as Sarah."

Rosalind was the infamous Sarah? Does that mean that the whole thing was a scam? Maybe he truly thought Sarah was being held hostage, but really it was just Rosalind playing games. How did the cops picking him up here factor into this? Do they have someone up high on their side? I feel sorry that he gave up everything for this Sarah, only to be a pawn in Rosalind's games.

"You keep using past tense," I say, realizing why she didn't want to bring it up. He's dead. And considering River didn't tell me about it, he must have done it. "He got plenty of chances," I say quietly. "You can't help some people."

And it's true. What goes around comes around.

He was given chances, even after coming here with a gun and shooting Jeremiah and trying to kill Romeo.

I think River must have been in a good mood that day.

When the bath is filled, I leave her to it, and find River sitting on our bed with his head in his hands, collecting himself.

"Are you okay?" I ask, sitting down next to him.

"Yeah, I'm just glad she was all right," he replies. "When she wasn't in the warehouse, inside I was freaking the fuck out. Luckily Jeremiah checked the back of that car. What a fucking stressful day. We trusted Rosalind, let her into our home, and look what she did. I think we need to be more careful about who we trust, whether they are family or not."

"What's going to happen to her?" I ask, absently rubbing his back.

"Well, I would have liked her dead, if I'm being honest, but I know Julianna would have been devastated, and she's pregnant, so we don't want to upset her. So we're handing Rosalind over to her father and putting it on him that he's responsible for anything she does from now on. And Cathy we handed to her son, Andrew." To his father. "And he and Romeo will decide what to do with her."

"It's a hard situation," I say, wincing. "Like Cathy's an old evil mastermind. What are you supposed to do with her? Put her in a home with high security or something?"

"She's not old enough for a home, unless we can

prove she has dementia or something. Maybe we can try to get her into a facility on the other side of the country. Or better yet, in another country."

That makes me laugh. "That sounds like a pretty good idea."

"Thank you for always being there for not just me, but for everyone else in the club, too," he says, kissing my cheek. "You are the best thing that has ever happened to me."

"You guys are my family now, too," I say, looking into his beautiful blue eyes. "And just like you'll do anything for me, I'll do anything for you. You are the love of my life, River. And I don't say that lightly."

"I think you already know you are the love of mine," he replies, pushing me back onto the bed and lying on top of me, careful to not put all his weight down. "I fucking love you so much, I never knew I could feel this way about anyone."

I brush the dark hair off his forehead and enjoy the moment of just being in love.

Because what a fucking magical place to be.

Chapter Twenty-Eight

River

The next day, while Bella goes to view some properties, I decide to go for a run, just to clear my head and process everything that has happened recently. It's been a lot, and I hate that Corey was dragged into this when she's still healing from what happened to Matthew. She doesn't deserve any of it, and Rosalind using Mom against her was a low blow.

It also shows me that no matter how much she says that she's okay and doesn't care about our mother, she obviously still does, because one text had her out running to her. And that breaks my fucking heart. Mom needs to reach out to her and be her mother, because no matter how much I'm there for her, nothing can replace the love of a mother or father. I've tried to stay out of it, but I'm definitely going to be speaking to Mom next time I visit her, because this needs to stop.

When I get back to the clubhouse, Romeo is out front cleaning his motorcycle. When he sees me, he stops what he's doing and comes over to me.

"Hey, there's something I wanted to ask you about," he says as I remove my earbuds. I know what he's going to say, and I guess there's no time like the present to get this out of the way.

"Yeah? What's up?" I ask, bracing myself.

"I wanted to talk about what Cathy said when we were in the warehouse. Something about how she has always known… What was she talking about?" he asks, brow furrowed.

Shifting my feet, I look down before staring him in the eye. "At Jeremiah's birthday, your mom got drunk and told me that Robert isn't my real father. Andrew is. It was some secret our mothers knew about. I haven't spoken to your dad, so I don't know if he knows, or his side of the story, but my mom confirmed that it's true. You and I apparently share the same father. So we're half brothers."

And cousins.

I have no idea how that works.

"What the fuck," Romeo says quietly, shaking his head. "How could they keep this from us all these years? And why didn't you tell me? You should have told me as soon as my mother told you."

"I know, I just was struggling processing it all," I admit, running my hand through my hair in frustration. "I didn't know how to tell you, I didn't know what to think. I only told Bella a few days ago, and then I was going to tell you."

He opens his mouth, then closes it. "Well, *I'm* at the processing stage now, so I need some time. And yeah. I wish you told me right away." He turns away from me and walks back inside.

"Fuck," I grit out, wanting to hit something.

I know how hard it must be for him. Firstly it means his dad cheated on his mom when she was pregnant with Romeo, and with his aunt, and yeah, he's right. I should have told him. He deserved to know the truth just as much as I did.

When Cathy said she knew, I wasn't surprised. She's the type who knows everything.

I go into the gym and punch the bag for a while, take a shower and then ask Bella if she wants to go out for lunch.

I need to get out of here.

Romeo is scarce for the next few days, and I give him that space. On day four, though, enough is enough.

"Are we ever going to talk about this?" I ask when he comes into the gym while I'm working out. "I'm done with this, Romeo. It's always been us two, and I want us to go back to how we were. I didn't want us to change and that's why I didn't even want to talk about what I'd heard."

And now things feel different, and I don't fucking like it.

"I'm not angry, I'm just... I don't know, okay? I

don't know how to handle this," he says, shrugging. "I spoke to my mother, and she said she never meant to tell you about it—it just happened because she was so drunk. So they were just never going to tell us. And when I asked Dad about it…"

"What did he say?" I press, as this is something that's been weighing heavily on my mind. What does Andrew say about all of this?

"He said he didn't know for sure, but he had a suspicion. But when Aunty Lisa didn't say anything to him, he assumed you were Robert's, because the timing was so close together," he explains, and when I really look at him, I notice how tired he appears, like he hasn't been getting much rest.

"It doesn't have to change anything," I tell him, getting off the weight machine and going over to him. "We are us, just like we've always been. You've always been like a brother to me, Romeo. This just makes it official."

"It means you are next in line to the MC, after my child," he says, scanning my face. "So where do you stand with all that? Because I want my child to lead, whether it's a boy or a girl. If I have a daughter, which Julianna thinks it will be, you could fight for leadership by sticking to the old ways."

"That's what you're worried about? I don't want the MC. If I have to stand up and lead one day, I can, sure. But I'm not gunning for that position, and I'd never take that away from any of your future children, no matter their gender. You know me, Romeo.

You know me. So stop second-guessing everything just because of what we found out," I say.

He nods. "You're right, I do know you. And I've always loved you like my brother."

He holds out his palm and we shake hands, and then we share a hug.

I hated fighting with him, and now we can move forward and deal with the hand we've been dealt.

Now I just need to tell Corey about it, and it's all out in the open.

And eventually, I'm going to have to face Andrew.

Chapter Twenty-Nine

Bella

"This week has been a shit show, and now I find out that River and I don't even have the same dads. I mean, what the fuck," Corey says, coming into my office and sitting down on the daybed. "I'm almost scared to find out what tomorrow is going to bring."

I swivel around in my chair. "He was as shocked, don't worry. And it still doesn't change anything for you both. You are still and always will be his baby sister."

"I know," she sighs, staring at her freshly done white fingernails. "It was just a shock. What other secrets is this family keeping? Actually, never mind, I don't even want to know. A whole cupboard of skeletons will probably fall out and crush us all."

I can't help but laugh. "You know what, I think you're right. It will be nice to have things a little drama-free for a while. No evil villain grannies or anything would be lovely."

One love betrayal is more than enough.

"Only our family," she sighs, standing up. "Can I do something for you for once? Get you something to eat or drink?"

She's so sweet, and obviously wants to do something nice for me. So even though I already have a fridge full of snacks and drinks, I say, "Yes, please, I would love a coffee. And maybe some of those shortbread biscuits Julianna bought the other day."

She beams as she walks out. "Okay, I'm on it."

Julianna finds her way into my office next—it's almost like it's become everyone's psychologist sessions. The poor thing looks upset, her eyes puffy and sad. And understandably so. Betrayal is a hell of a weapon, and it's one that can take anyone down.

"I can't believe Rosalind did this to me," she says, sitting in the spot Corey just vacated. "I should have known that she didn't forgive me and Romeo for being together. I thought she got over it and wanted to make amends, but boy, was I wrong. I don't ever want to see her again."

"What is your dad going to do with her?" I ask gently, wishing there was something I could do to help. "What if this is something she's never going to let go, like with Cathy? I think losing Johnny Boy to Libby just pushed her over the edge even further, so they feel like they have nothing to lose."

"They just want to bring down everyone around

them. It's pathetic. My parents don't know what to do with her. At the end of the day, that's their daughter. But Romeo told them she gets one chance and one chance only, because the next time the MC will be dealing with her themselves. I know I'm the only reason he was so lenient, but I just hope I don't come to regret it," she says, scrubbing her hands down her face. "You can't choose your family. I just don't know how I got paired with Dumb and Dumber."

I choke with laughter. "It's not your fault—you were a good sister to her. Unfortunately you can't control other people and their intentions. But we can make sure that we don't trust them again. Fool me once, shame on you…"

"Fool me twice, shame on me," she finishes, nodding. "Yeah, you're right. I just don't understand how she can be filled with such hatred. She only dated Romeo for a few months, and I didn't know about that when I met and fell in love with him. If I did know I probably wouldn't have gone near him, because who the hell wants their sister's sloppy seconds?"

I cover my mouth with my hand, trying to contain my amusement.

"But no, I didn't know, and I fell head over heels in love with him, and here we are. With my sister now apparently wanting to kill him for deciding to marry and have a child with me," she continues with her rant. "And because I'm pregnant I can't even slap her across the face like I want to."

"I can do it for you, if you like," I offer, and her lip twitches. "I mean, Corey did."

She grins. "True."

Corey returns about twenty minutes later, with a mug of coffee and cookies. "Sorry I took so long. I ran into River, who wanted to have another discussion about me and him not having the same father." She places them on my desk and then goes and sits next to Julianna. "And how are you doing?"

"My sister tried to kill my husband," Julianna tells her.

Corey nods. "Yes, I was there. Your sister kidnapped me."

Julianna hugs her with a sigh. "I'm so sorry, Corey. From now on that bitch isn't coming anywhere near us and our family."

I move next to them and hug them too, just as River sticks his head into the room, smiling when he sees all of us. "You guys are pretty damn cute."

"Just feeling sorry for ourselves," Julianna says, looking up at him. "You know, I always thought of you as his baby's uncle, but you actually really are his uncle. That's pretty cool."

"Thanks," he replies, looking down at her stomach. "And I never thought about it, but… I like that. I would have loved that baby regardless, though, blood or not."

"I know," she replies, smiling. "Do you want to come and sit with us? There's room for one more on this daybed."

He smiles and comes to sit next to me on the end, taking up the space of two people, and as always making us feel safe.

"So what happens next?" I ask them.

"Next we make sure that we're all okay, safe and happy," Julianna replies. "And we have a baby. And we don't let anyone else hurt us."

"And we trust each other more," Corey says, looking at her brother.

"And we don't make out with men in front of people's brothers," he replies in a dry tone. "The next time I see you kissing someone better be at your wedding."

Corey rolls her eyes, and I decide to change the subject.

"Who is hungry?"

Chapter Thirty

River

"Dad loves the idea of sending Cathy away to a home on the other side of the country," Romeo says. "He has some connections there and knows someone who would keep a close eye on her to make sure she doesn't leave the private home." We're about to go for an overdue ride as a group, and I for one can't wait. "He's heading out to look into it in a few days."

"And Rosalind?" I ask, wondering about the second wicked witch.

Romeo scowls at the mere mention of her name. "Yeah, I'd like to see what they do with her, but I'm guessing it's going to be a big fat fucking nothing because she's Daddy's little girl. I'm giving him that respect as our ex-president and Julianna's father, for now. But I said what I mean—if she steps out of line again, we will be handling her. I suggested that he marry her off somewhere, because she's not wanted around here. And the Angels love marrying their women off, so what's the big deal now?"

I laugh, because he does have a point. Julianna was meant to marry Victor at her father's decree, but obviously that was scrapped when Romeo married her instead, and Victor...died. So why not marry off Rosalind? To someone who doesn't know what a snake she is.

Bella stays back with Julianna, Corey and Jag while the rest of us head out for a taste of freedom. It's been a while since we had a ride like this, and I enjoy every second of it. The only thing that would make it better would be to have Bella on the back of my bike.

When we make our first stop at a biker bar, I see Damon pull up to join us. I haven't seen him since we saved Corey, and I know I should say something to him. I wait until we're inside at the bar ordering a drink.

"Hey, I just wanted to say thank you for your help that day," I say, clearing my throat. "I could tell you did care about her and would have done anything to save her. So thank you."

"You don't need to thank me," he replies, gray eyes giving nothing away. "You aren't the only person in the world who can care about her."

He takes his drink and walks off, leaving me feeling like an asshole. But I said what I came to say, and yeah, I probably could have added in an apology, but I still don't think he should have been kissing my sister out in the open like he would with any woman. She's not any woman.

"He's a good guy," Romeo says, smirking. "But no one will be good enough for Corey, will they?"

"I don't know, I'll let you know if I ever meet anyone," I reply, taking a sip of ice-cold beer.

Romeo laughs and sits down on the barstool. "I feel sorry for whoever ends up with her, let me tell you that much."

"You could be having a daughter soon, so I wouldn't say anything if I were you," I reply, grinning.

He sighs, and rubs the back of his neck, suddenly stressed. "I think it's going to be a boy, but if it's a girl who looks like Julianna, I'll be in deep shit. Are you and Bella going to get married? Have kids?"

Now I'm the one sweating. "Yes. I mean, I know she's the one for me. But I don't think I'm in any rush to have kids. I've got my hands pretty full with everything else that's been going on right now."

"Uh-huh," he replies, amused. "And the marriage side of it?"

"I'll get there," I say, clearing my throat. The truth is I never thought I'd be a man getting married and having kids. But Bella has changed all of that for me. I do picture myself doing those things with her, but that doesn't mean I'm ready to rush in right now and propose. "We've only just started living together, so let's wait a few months."

"Women don't like to wait," he reminds me, arching his brow. "If I were you, I'd start looking at rings and thinking about these things."

Romeo and Julianna got married very quickly and in secret, so I don't think he's the one to go to for advice on this one. As if reading my mind, he says, "When you know, you know."

And I do know.

But there's also no rush. I will get there when I'm ready. Or when she's ready, I suppose. Shit, I suppose that's another conversation that needs to be had.

I know that ultimately I'd give her whatever she wanted.

It's dark outside by the time I get home, and I feel like today has filled my cup. But I'm also excited to get home and see what Bella is up to.

Fuck, who am I?

I've gotten used to having her around, to coming home to her, and I'm just enjoying these moments every day. I've gone from seeing her a few nights a week, if that, and sometimes having no contact for days, to being with her every moment I can.

I don't know what she's done to me.

I find them all playing pool in the games room, Corey sitting at the bar having a drink while Bella and Julianna are deep in a game.

Bella beams when she sees me, and throws her arms around me. "There you are. I'm about to beat Julianna, I'm glad you're here to witness this moment."

Julianna drinks some pickle juice while she waits for her turn. "Yeah, yeah, keep rubbing it in."

Romeo comes to find his wife, picks her up and carries her out. Julianna laughs and pokes her tongue out.

"Wait, I'm about to beat her!" Bella calls out, reaching for her.

Luckily Corey steps in to play. After she wins, we have dinner and then go to bed.

It was a normal day, with no guns, violence, kidnapping or drama. A day that started and ended with Bella in my arms.

I must be getting old, because it was pretty fucking great.

I think I could get used to this.

Chapter Thirty-One

Bella

Five Months Later

I'm on my knees in front of River in the shower, my eyes closed as the water hits my face, my hand braced on his thigh. I suck his cock deeply into my mouth, as far as I can take him and back again. He's a big man, so there's no way in hell I can fit the whole thing, but I get an A for effort. His body is incredible, all corded muscle and hard lines. I could stare up at him all fucking day. He threads his fingers in my hair and leans back up against the tiles, while I taste the very essence of him.

I reach down to gently cup his balls when there's a loud banging on the door. I look up, pulling myself out of the sexual daze I'm in, and stare into annoyed blue eyes.

"Someone better be dying," he says in a husky

tone, helping me up and then leaving the shower. I stay under the hot water while he goes to see what's going on.

"Julianna's in labor," he yells through the door, and I instantly turn the shower off and jump out. "They're leaving now, but Romeo said to come to the hospital."

"Of course," I say, quickly getting ready. I can't believe the time has come—excitement fills me at the thought of meeting my new niece or nephew. We rush to the car and I pick up some flowers from the hospital gift shop on the way in.

When I knock at the door of her hospital room, Julianna tells both of us to come in, but River lingers at the door. "What are you doing?"

"I'll wait here," he says, gesturing for me to go in. "You're her cousin, but I don't think she'd want me in there."

I hesitate but leave him outside and go in to check on her. "I'm glad you're here. Where's River?" Julianna asks when she sees me.

"He's outside—he wasn't sure if you wanted him in," I say, placing the flowers next to her bed.

"Thank you." She beams, looking at them. "They are beautiful."

"You're welcome." I take her hand in mine. She's wearing a blue hospital robe and has a monitor on her belly, to check the baby's heart rate.

"Romeo, can you go and get him?" she asks her husband, who gets up instantly. She had told River and me she'd like us both in the room, if we'd be okay with that.

"How are you?" I ask her.

"Good now—they gave me an epidural," she says, eyes going wide. "If you came here a little earlier you probably would have heard me screaming down the hallway. It hurt, Bella. So fucking bad. Like knives stabbing me in my lower stomach."

"And the epidural stopped that?" I ask, intrigued. I make a mental note to definitely get one of those when it's my time to have a baby.

"Yeah. I'm only five centimeters dilated, so it might be some time. Or it might come on quick; we will just have to wait and see."

Romeo and River come back in and stand around her, like a unit. After a few hours of our company, she's finally dilated enough to push.

"Okay, River, you stay by my head," she says, making me laugh. I hold one hand, River holds the other and Romeo stays down near the crowning vagina side to witness the birth of his child firsthand.

The epidural must be wearing off, because Julianna starts to cry out in pain.

"You can do this," I say. "Use each contraction, go with it, don't fight against it."

Yes, I did some reading prior to coming here, wanting to know what the hell I'm supposed to say and do that might be helpful other than just telling her to breathe. Her nails score my palm, but I don't mind. It's nothing compared with what she's going through right now.

"I can see the head!" Romeo calls out, hand on her leg. "Oh my God, you are doing amazing."

River looks a little traumatized but lets her hold his hand and squeeze the shit out of it with her nails, like she's doing to me. He even feeds her ice chips when she asks, and rubs her arm in silent comfort.

And then we hear her heart-wrenching warrior cry, and then the wails of the baby. Romeo all but delivers the baby, catching it as it comes out, the midwife and doctor on each side of him helping. Aside from Romeo, we'd all assumed it would have been a girl—after all, the Callistos haven't had a boy in their line for as long as we can remember. So when Romeo announces it, I'm in complete shock.

"It's a boy," he says, choking up with emotion. "A beautiful baby boy."

"A boy?" Julianna repeats, sounding confused. She looks over at me and we both share our surprise.

A boy.

Romeo cuts the cord, and the doctor checks over the baby quickly before giving him to Julianna to hold. River and I leave to give them their private moment, and so Julianna can have some skin-on-skin contact with her newborn son.

We sit outside in the waiting room, wrapped in each other's arms.

"When do you think you'll want a baby?" River

asks, tucking my hair back behind my ear. "You said that you wanted them, but never said when."

"Did that scare you off having kids?" I tease. "Because I'm pretty sure it's the woman doing all of the work."

He grins and kisses my temple. "The women do the work, the men do the worrying."

"I don't know, maybe in a year? How about you?" I ask, wondering where his mind is at. Is he asking me because he's ready or because he's not? Or is he just bracing himself for when the time comes?

"A year sounds good," he agrees. "I just want you to be happy, and not feel like you're missing out on anything because you chose me to fall in love with."

"That wasn't a choice. I couldn't have stopped myself if I tried." I grin, resting my head on his shoulder. "But it's not all about me and my timeline. We're a team, and we can compromise so we're both happy."

"I think a year is good. Gives us some time with just us, before we add to our family."

"Did you ever think you'd be having this conversation?" I ask.

"No," he laughs. "Nor did I think I'd ever be in a room with a woman giving birth."

We go back in to see baby Julian, who is absolutely gorgeous, with dark hair and his dad's brown eyes. Seeing River holding him makes me question if I can wait the year I just requested.

"You look very nice with that baby," I say, and Julianna laughs.

"Uh-oh, you're in trouble now, River."

Instead of freaking out like I thought he would, he smiles and looks down at the baby. My heart flutters at the sight of him. He'd be an amazing dad, I've always known that, albeit a little overprotective.

But I'd balance that out in him.

"I just thought I'd let you know that his full name is Julian River Montanna," Julianna adds, smiling happily. "And we'd like for both of you to be his godparents."

River looks away, rubbing his eyes. It's the first time I've seen him cry. "I'd love that."

"Me, too," I reply, hugging my cousin. "And now I know it's a boy, I get to go shopping."

I hug Romeo, and River does the same.

And then we leave them to get acquainted with their new bundle of joy.

Our godson.

Chapter Thirty-Two

River

Now that they have a baby, Romeo and Julianna get their own little place, but because they will still be at the clubhouse a lot, we also set up a nursery and baby-proof the house for them. Bella and I surprise them with the fully stocked nursery, and we get Corey, who is amazing at painting, to do a mural on the wall. She paints an ocean theme, with a whale shark, octopus and manta ray. It looks fucking wonderful. Bella went out and bought wooden letters so we can put his name up on the wall.

Julian River.

What a strong name, and it means the world to me that they named him after me.

After three nights in the hospital, they come to the clubhouse and we surprise them with the nursery. Julianna cries, and Romeo gets all emotional, hugging me.

"It's nicer than the one we have set up at our new place," Julianna says, wiping her eyes. "Now we might as well just live here."

"We wanted him to be comfortable when he is here," Bella says, carrying Julian against her chest and gently rocking him.

"Corey, I had no idea you were so talented," Romeo says to my sister, wrapping his arm around her and pulling her against him.

"Thank you." She beams, looking over at her work. "I'm glad you like it."

"We love it," he replies.

Bella puts Julian in his new crib, and Julianna takes photos of him doing things like sleeping and breathing.

Jag comes into the room and nods for us to come out with him.

"What is it?" I ask.

"Rosalind is here. She said she wants to see her nephew. Jeremiah is with her out front," he says quietly, glancing inside the nursery. "Can I go and see the baby?"

"Yeah, go ahead. Keep them inside while I deal with this," Romeo says, and Jag goes in while Romeo and I head outside to see the woman who, only a few months ago, tried to have him killed.

"I can't believe she came here," he grits out. "I don't want her to upset Julianna."

"What are you going to do?" I ask as he opens the door and steps outside. "What is the game plan?"

"I have no fucking idea," he replies, but we both walk up to her.

"Finally," she says, rolling her eyes.

We tried to get her dad to marry her off, but he didn't. Instead he promised that she wouldn't try anything again, and if she did then we could handle it however we wanted. Cathy was sent away to a private home in the end, supervised by a trusted friend of the MC, so we won half the war. Unfortunately the half we lost is standing right in front of us. She's been lying low these last few months, where I wish she would have stayed.

"You aren't welcome here, Rosalind. Leave. And don't come back, or you're not going to like what happens to you," Romeo says, narrowing his eyes. "Leave."

"I'm here to see my sister and congratulate her on the baby," she replies, crossing her arms over her chest. "I don't want any problems—I just want to see my nephew."

"You lost that right when you did what you did—"

"I wanted to kill *you*, not Julianna or the baby," she fires back, cutting him off. "I'm not a threat to them. Just let my sister come out and see me."

"Do you think she wants to see you?" he asks, voice getting louder. "She doesn't. Now leave or I will personally be escorting you home."

The door opens and Corey walks out. When she sees Rosalind, she storms right up to her, and does what we've all wanted to but haven't because she's a woman: she punches her in the face. An upgrade from her slap from last time.

Rosalind touches her jaw, wincing in pain.

"Get out of here, you stupid bitch. You are not ever welcome here. We are a family, and you are not part of it," Corey says, getting right up close to her.

Rosalind steps back, her face full of fury, and gets back in her car and drives away.

That must have felt good for Corey, taking her power back after what Rosalind did to her. "You okay?" I ask, feeling proud.

"Never better," she replies, turning around and walking back inside.

I share a look with Romeo, and then do the same.

That bitch isn't messing with us and ours ever again.

When I get a moment alone with Julianna in the kitchen, I quietly ask her an important question. "Has Bella ever mentioned to you what kind of engagement ring she'd like? She hasn't ever given me any hints and now I don't know what I'm supposed to be looking at. I know she wears gold, but what diamond shape do you think she'd like?"

"Oh my goodness," she whisper-yells, and then does a happy dance. "I am so damn excited right now! I never thought…wow. Okay, in fact I do know the answer to this. She's always wanted a pear-shaped diamond."

"Perfect," I say, relieved. "Do not say anything."

"Of course I won't," she replies, offended. "I am

so happy for you both, River. You both deserve happiness, and I can see how much you truly love each other. Who would have thought? I still remember the first time both of you met. I tried warning her away from you, but she didn't listen to me. And for once I'm glad that she didn't."

"Me, too," I reply, remembering that fateful night. "Although you were probably right to warn her."

She tilts her head to the side, studying me. "You're the best thing that's ever happened to her."

She then gets up on her tiptoes and kisses me on the cheek, before leaving the room. I pull out my phone and look at some different rings.

If pear is what Bella wants, pear is what she's going to get.

And the bigger the rock, the better.

I only plan on doing this once in my life, so it needs to be fucking amazing.

Chapter Thirty-Three

Bella

A few weeks pass before I decide to rent out my house. It's just sitting there, empty, and it makes no sense for me to keep it that way, so we pack it all up and I permanently move into the clubhouse. I know it's a big step, because it means I have no backup plan, but I'm one hundred percent sure this is where I want to be. I love being with River every day, and not just him but also the rest of the MC. I am going to miss my garden, but River told me I'm welcome to plant whatever I want at the clubhouse.

My parents finally come back from their adventures and meet River, and although they don't love the fact that I'm living in the clubhouse, they don't really have a choice because this is what I've decided to do.

"You don't have any privacy, though, Bella," Mom

comments, frowning. "Why don't you both move into your house?"

"River needs to be at the clubhouse, so that's where I want to be, too," I say, glancing around my old, now-empty bedroom. "And I'll get more income from the rent, too. It's a win-win situation."

My mother sighs heavily and goes into the kitchen to get some water, with me following behind her. "You're unmarried and living with a Devils MC member. I don't think this is how I thought your life would go."

I purse my lips, and suddenly I'm unable to hold my tongue. "They are my family. You and Dad are barely around, and that's fine, you can both go and enjoy your life. But don't tell me how to live mine."

She leaves unhappy, but I honestly don't care. She can't come out of nowhere and tell me how things should be. It just doesn't work like that.

River isn't home when I return to the clubhouse after dropping my keys off to the real estate agent. But I can tell you who is here.

"Oh, hello," I say to Andrew, the old president of the Devils MC, and Romeo's father.

And River's father.

"Hello, Bella," he says. "I was hoping to catch River, but looks like he just went out."

Romeo walks out of the gym, still shirtless, and sees us both standing there. "Dad, when did you get back?"

"About an hour ago. Never let your mother plan such a long trip overseas again."

"What are you doing here?"

I excuse myself and leave to go into my bedroom, but not before I hear some of their conversation. Okay, I end up waiting in the hallway and listening.

"I came to speak to River."

"You let him grow up thinking that monster was his father," Romeo says, and I can hear the gruffness in his tone. "Why didn't you speak to Lisa and find out the truth?"

Silence for a few moments before Andrew replies. "I never knew for sure. It was complicated. Victoria was already pregnant with you, even though we hadn't been dating long. Lisa was with Robert. But I'm here now, and I want to apologize to him and to you. I should have known, and I should have demanded the truth be known."

"Yes, you should have," Romeo snaps. "It would have caused a lot less trauma for River, who always thought he was just like his father."

"He is—he's more like me than that bastard."

"With no thanks to you," Romeo replies. "He carries around the guilt of what happened to Robert."

"Well, he shouldn't. Robert deserved what he got. In fact, we should have done something sooner, so that Lisa and the kids could have had a better life."

"Why didn't you come to speak to River sooner?" Romeo asks.

Andrew stretches his neck from side to side. "This

wasn't exactly a conversation to have on the phone, Romeo. I came here as soon as I could."

I hear River's voice as he walks inside. "Hey. What's going on?"

I decide to leave and stop eavesdropping so he can have a private conversation with his father, and brother.

Okay, I leave just so I definitely don't get caught listening.

When River comes into the bedroom an hour or so later, he tells me that Andrew apologized to him, and doesn't want to keep any secrets. He wants to openly acknowledge him as his son.

"Why did he take so long to come around?" I ask. River seems to forgive Andrew but I can't. Not yet.

"Well, he never knew the truth—he suspected. Ignorance is bliss, I guess." He shrugs. That feels like the motto for the last year. But if I've learned anything, it's that knowing the truth matters more. "And Victoria asked that he keeps his distance. She felt horrible for telling me and I think she wanted to ignore her guilt for a while."

What a family!

"He seemed genuine about it, but I don't know. He was more than happy to dust it under the rug all of these years," he says, sighing. "The 'it' being me."

"I guess it's more complicated than that, isn't it, with him dating your mom's sister, and then your mom getting into a relationship with a new man, too," I say, sitting on his lap and holding him. "But it's nice he wants to make amends now."

"Yeah, it is, and it's nice to have it all out in the open," he admits. "I'm glad that things can calm down now. And speaking of, I was thinking, how about we go away for a night or two?"

"Where to?" I ask, excitedly.

"I'll book us a cabin somewhere, and we can eat, drink and sightsee," he suggests, kissing my neck. "And be as loud as we want without you worrying that everyone can hear us."

I laugh. "That sounds nice. Let's do it."

"Good," he replies, turning my face to him and kissing me. His fingers brush my nipples and I moan softly.

I would have thought that living together we'd be having less sex, but no, we are still firmly in the honeymoon stage, and still can't get enough of each other.

He pushes me back onto the bed, lifts my dress and pulls down my red panties, growling when he sees them. "You've been wearing this around all day? Fuck."

And then his mouth is on my pussy, his hands on my thighs, and I'm lying back and enjoying every second.

He slides a finger inside of me at the same time he sucks on my clit, and it almost sends me over the edge. When he pulls back, I know he doesn't want me to come yet, but then he shouldn't be so fucking talented with his mouth and hands.

And his cock.

Trifecta.

His puts his tongue back on me, circling my clit just how I like it, and then it's all over, and I come with his name on my lips, my hips jerking off the bed as wave after wave of pleasure hits me.

Afterward, he gets up and wipes his mouth with the back of his hand, and moves to stand.

"Where the hell do you think you're going?" I ask, getting up on shaky legs and pushing him back onto the bed. "I'm not done with you yet."

He grins, flashing his straight white teeth, and pulls off his shirt. I take a moment to enjoy his muscular body as I undo his zipper and pull his jeans down, exposing his thick, hard cock.

And then I take him into my mouth and let the fun begin again.

Chapter Thirty-Four

River

I wish I could say that I felt calm, but I'm freaking the fuck out. The box is burning a hole in my pocket, and I just hope that she says yes.

Please, let her say yes.

We arrived at our luxury resort this morning, and have since looked around and had some lunch. I then booked us in for a couples massage, and while we are gone from our villa, I've organized a private dinner to be set up just for us. I asked for rose petals to be laid on the ground, trailing from the entrance and ending in a big heart, which is where I will get down on one knee. I want to make it as romantic as possible, and for someone like me, who is more comfortable with violence than romance, it's been a bit stressful. But for Bella, I would do anything, and she deserves a proper, romantic proposal, with lots of effort and thought involved.

Holding hands, we walk back to the villa, admiring the beauty of the resort. "I thought you said you'd get a cabin—I wasn't expecting anything as fancy as this," she says, glancing around. "It's beautiful here. I love it."

"I'm glad," I reply, touching the box in my pocket to make sure it's there for the millionth time. "I wanted to spoil you a little, and after looking online, a cabin wasn't going to cut it."

"You always spoil me," she replies, pointing to some beautiful flowers. "How pretty."

"Yes, gorgeous," I reply, staring at her.

"That massage was the best I think I've ever had. I feel so relaxed," she says, smiling up at me. "I love you, you know that? Thanks for bringing me here."

"I love you, too," I say, stopping to open the door to our villa for her to enter before me. She walks inside and then stops when she sees the rose petals, in the shape of a heart, and trailing around the beautifully set dinner table.

"Oh my God," she whispers. "River, this is beautiful."

She turns around, her eyes wide and a smile on her face, and I drop to one knee before her.

"Bella, you are the love of my life, my soulmate, and I want to spend the rest of my life with you. Will you make me the happiest man alive by marrying me?" I ask, my fingers trembling as I hold the box open for her to see the ring.

"Yes, of course I will," she replies, her eyes tearing up with happiness. I slide the ring on her finger, and she looks at it with wonder. "That is the most stunning ring I've ever seen in my life."

Thank fuck.

All my nerves disappear and I stand up and kiss her. She said yes, she's mine for fucking ever.

I pull out her chair for her and we both sit, and our dinner is served to us, course by course. Just the two of us, under the moonlight, surrounded by rose petals, our private pool lit up with romantic dim lighting.

"I can't believe you did all this," she says, looking down at her ring in awe. "I can't stop smiling."

I put on some Ed Sheeran for her to listen to, and we finish our dinner and then dance together, enjoying everything about this moment.

It's the happiest moment of my life.

The next few days we spend at the villa, living our best lives, making love, eating and swimming. It's perfect. Bella wears her ring proudly, and I couldn't love her and our time together any more.

I have a fiancée.

That's why as soon we get home to the clubhouse, and the police show up to take me in for questioning, you can imagine how pissed off I am. I've been living in a romantic bubble the last few days, only to come home to this bullshit.

"We'd like to ask you some questions on the disappearance of Robert Montanna," the officer says, escorting me to the car. The look in the cops' eyes is not friendly. They think I murdered him.

Fuck.

I was kind of thinking they were coming after me for the murder of Mark, or maybe Victor, so this one caught me by surprise.

I can see the panic in Bella's eyes as I'm driven away, and I curse the cops for their timing, and my ass-hole stepfather for still ruining my life from the grave.

Because I did kill Robert Montanna.

But how the fuck are they going to prove it?

They sit me in the examination room and try the good cop, bad cop method to get a confession, or any other information out of me. They can try as hard as they like. Getting confessions out of people is what I do for fun, and none of their legal mind games are going to work, but go ahead and let them try.

"We got a tip that you might know what happened to Robert, so we just want to talk to you about it," the nice cop says, sitting down opposite me.

Who would know this? Romeo? No, he wouldn't. Bella? No. She would never do that to me. I trust her with my life.

But who would say something now? Andrew? Now that the cat's out of the bag, maybe he wants me out of the way?

The cop pours me a glass of water. "Were you close with your father?"

"Not really, but last I heard that wasn't a crime. Do you have any evidence to back up this tip?" I ask, curious as to whether they can keep me, or if this is just them grasping at straws to try to pin someone for Robert's murder.

"This is just an interview," she replies, which means they have nothing. And as they should, because I covered my tracks extremely well.

After Robert beat my mother so bad for the last time, she was put in a coma to relieve the swelling in her head. That's when she lost the sight in her eye.

And that is when I went to his house and killed him.

We fought first, until he was a bloodied mess, and then with the last hit, he fell back and knocked his head on the tiles. He died quickly, and I wish it wasn't the case, but fate took it out of my hands. It was hard getting rid of his body, I have to admit. But I did what I needed to and covered my tracks. I burned the body, and there are no traces of him remaining.

When my mother got out of the hospital, she didn't know what had happened, but I told her Robert had left and I hadn't seen him. I told her that maybe he went to visit his firstborn son from another woman, Tatum, who he rarely saw. I don't know if she's aware of the truth, but I think that deep down inside she does, because she hasn't been looking over her shoulder waiting for his return.

She knows he isn't coming back to hurt anyone ever again. I made sure of that. "Okay, well, I haven't seen him in years. We all assumed he went to stay with family out east," I say. "I didn't even know he was dead. Has his body been found, then?"

The cop says nothing, which means again, no.

Bad cop steps in then, a large burly-looking man, and leans over me. "We know you did it. Just tell us the truth, and we can make a deal to get you less time. Tell us where his body is."

"I did not do anything," I tell him. "I'm not saying anything else until my lawyer gets here. Because I don't like these accusations that you are making."

They aren't going to find the body.

I do my own cleanups, and I'm thorough as fuck.

Good cop takes over, because of course they don't want me calling a lawyer. Especially when my lawyer is Jaxon fucking Bentley, one of the best criminal defense lawyers in our county.

"I'd like to call my lawyer, please," I say, staying calm and collected. I'd also like to be with Bella to make sure that she is okay. She must be so worried right now, and asking a lot of questions.

She doesn't know what happened to Robert.

But she does know what I'm capable of.

Chapter Thirty-Five

Bella

"This is not the welcome home I was expecting," I cry, wiping my tears away. As soon as River was taken away, I went to get help from the MC. "Did you get in contact with his lawyer?"

Romeo nods. "Yes, he's on his way to the station now. Don't stress, they don't have anything on him. You don't think Rosalind is the one who did the anonymous call, do you?"

"I wouldn't put anything past her," Corey says, arms wrapped around herself in a protective cocoon. "Is this my fault, because I punched her?"

"No, it's not your fault," I tell her, frowning. "And it's all going to be okay."

I take a deep breath, in and out, to try to calm myself. It better fucking be okay, because right now we're meant to be celebrating our engagement, not dealing with this.

Julianna gives me a big hug. "I know it's awful timing, but congratulations. And I did notice your big-ass ring. It pretty much takes up half your hand."

I laugh through my tears. "Thank you. I was so excited to come home and tell you all about it, but then this happened. He will be okay, right? What if they lock him up?"

I honestly don't know what I'd do. I'd be devastated. I'm not cut out to be a prison wife.

"It will be okay, I promise. Let's not stress until we've spoken to his lawyer, okay? And you can still tell me all about the proposal; it will distract you," Julianna says, leading me to the living room and sitting down on the couch with me. Corey joins us, and I tell them about the proposal, the rose petals and all the effort he went to.

"That is so sweet," Julianna says, hand on her heart.

"Who knew he had it in him," Corey says, sounding extremely impressed. "Well done to him. I can't wait to congratulate him when this whole murder fiasco is done with."

She says it lightly, but I'm not sure if it's because she knows he didn't do it, or she's just playing it off so she doesn't have to deal with the reality of it herself. Maybe she's the optimistic sort.

Updating them does distract me, but it just makes me miss him and worry even more.

Dammit.

Julianna gives me baby Julian to try to cheer me up. "Here, hold him."

Looking into his little brown eyes, my heart does melt. I keep him close and rock him back and forth until he falls asleep.

"Any updates?" I ask Romeo when he comes into the room.

"Yes, I spoke to our lawyer. The police are trying to keep him, but they have nothing to keep him on. Apparently all they have is an anonymous tip and that's it. No body, no evidence, just a phone call. They are dreaming. He will be home by tonight, don't worry," he assures me, reaching down and taking Julian to put in his crib.

I sag back onto the leather couch, feeling hopeful. I don't know why this would resurface when Robert has been gone for years.

"Robert was the one who did that to your mom's eye, right?" I say to Corey, who nods slowly. I don't necessarily want her to know that River all but told me what happened.

"Yeah, Mom was in the hospital. She had to be put into a coma for swelling on her brain. And when she got out, Dad was gone. She's lost vision in one of her eyes because of how badly he beat her. We were all glad when he went missing, and our lives have been much better since then. He was awful. I don't know why she married and had two kids with him."

"She had two *beautiful* kids with him," I say, thinking of her and her brother Matthew. It wasn't their fault their dad was a piece of shit. And River too, because he still thought he was his father that whole time. "So I'm glad she did, or else you wouldn't be here and I'd never have a little sister."

Corey smiles and shrugs. "Yeah, I guess you're right. She should have left the first time he laid his hands on her, though. I don't know why she stayed. And I don't know why anyone didn't try to help her leave. I mean, maybe they did and we just didn't know. I guess it must have been hard with him being the son of the MC president, no one would have wanted to side with her."

"I think it's hard to consider unless you are in that situation," I say, waiting to see if she adds anything about River potentially being the one who either killed or somehow got rid of Robert, but she doesn't.

"I know," she replies, sighing. "And it doesn't change anything wondering why she did what she did. I just want my brother to be back home, and safe."

"Are you sure we shouldn't go to the police station and wait?" I ask, not for the first time.

"There's no point," I'm told, and, "He will call us when he's out."

As it gets late, I question if he's going to come home today, but at ten I get the call from him.

"Hello?" I say quickly. "River?" I'm sitting in the bathtub, steam filling the room.

"Yes, I'm on the way home now."

"Thank God," I say, closing my eyes in relief. "And that's it?"

"I don't know," he replies, sounding tired. "They

don't have any evidence right now, so unless they find something to bring me in again, I'd say that I'm good. I'll see you soon. Love you."

"Love you, too."

I'm still in the bath when he gets back, so he undresses and gets in with me. The hot water spills over the edge as he sits down, and then I move so my back is to his chest, with his arms around me.

"I was scared," I admit.

"I'm sorry," he says, kissing my cheek. "It was unexpected. But it's okay, I'm home, and they don't have anything on me other than suspicion."

I pause, and then just decide to ask him. "Did you have something to do with him going missing?"

I know we spoke about this before, and he said he would tell me, but once it's out there, he wouldn't be able to unsay it.

I wasn't ready before, but I think that I am now.

And deep inside, I already know the answer.

He stays quiet for a few moments, but then says, "Yes, I did. And I don't regret it."

Shit.

"I know why you did it," I say softly, resting my head back against him. "Thank you for being honest with me."

River, forever the protector.

"I will always be honest with you, Bella. There's some things I'd have liked to protect you from hearing, but the closer we get, I guess everything done in the dark will come to light. I just hope that it doesn't stop you from loving me," he replies, kissing the back of my neck. "As long as you know I'd never do anything to hurt you, ever. No matter what. Even if we broke up, I'd still protect you from afar, and be there for you if you ever needed me."

"We won't break up," I say, lifting my ring. "We're stuck together now. You just need to not go to prison, please."

He laughs. "I'll try my best. And I've made it this far without doing any hard time."

When we are done we get out of the bath, get dry and get into bed.

Not the engagement announcement I had planned, but as long as he's next to me, I don't care.

I'll take it as it is.

And as he is.

Chapter Thirty-Six

River

Feeling confident that no one will ever find enough evidence to incriminate me for Robert's death, I move on with my life and hope that whoever called the police minds their own business and shuts up about it. Obviously it could be Rosalind, or Granny Dearest making calls from the home she's in. Either one wouldn't surprise me. We'll just have to hope they both find some purpose in their lives that doesn't include trying to bring us down with their petty ways.

But some people never change.

Romeo tells me to keep a low profile and stay out of trouble, so that's what I plan to do. I just hope trouble doesn't come looking for me.

I'd hoped that Bella would never hear me confirm what I did to Robert—doing what I did to my own so-called father is pretty dark, even for me—but I couldn't go through him hurting my mother again. He needed to be taken care of, to keep everyone safe.

And trust me when I say he wasn't a good man and is one hundred percent in hell right now.

Maybe I'll see him there one day.

We have a club meeting, including the Angels as well, since even though we still have our own club-houses, we are one club. This is the first time I've seen Damon in a while, and I wonder what happened with him and Corey. She hasn't said anything, and I haven't wanted to ask.

"So as you know, we've had a lot of shit going on recently," Romeo says from the head of the table. "And I want to thank everyone for always being there and doing whatever needs to be done without any fucking complaint. As everyone knows, we had our son, Julian, which is why Julianna isn't here tonight, but usually she would be. Is there anything anyone would like to bring up or discuss?"

"Prospects," Damon says. "I know we have Jag, but I'd like to bring in a few more if we can, for the Angels clubhouse."

"You have anyone in mind?" Romeo asks him.

"No, but I'd like some younger members brought in, if Julianna agrees with that."

"I'll ask her about that, but I don't think it would be an issue," Romeo says, looking around the table.

A few other men speak up about different concerns, and Romeo talks it out with them. He then surprises me by what he says next.

"I just wanted to tell everyone that we've found out that River is my brother—we share the same father. It was a shock to us all, but I've always loved him like a brother anyway. This is just me officially letting you all know, so you can all stop fucking gossiping about it."

There is silence for a few seconds, before everyone cheers.

It's now all out in the open, no more dirty secrets. I feel...content.

We all head outside for some beer and music, and the women bring out food while I light the bonfire for us all. It's nice to have everyone around, even the members from the Angels. We are one. And I need to remember that when I see Damon. I suppose Corey could do worse.

"How good does the grazing platter look?" Bella says, pointing to the table. "It's a piece of art, I'm telling you."

"It looks amazing," I say, my hand wandering down to land on the curve of her ass. "But not as good as you."

Club members keeps coming up to congratulate us, and it feels more like a do-over engagement announcement than a club party. I hope she can feel the love in the room like I can.

"Can I get you a drink?" I ask, nuzzling against her. "Or something to eat?"

"I'm okay," she replies, wrapping her arms around my neck. I have to lower myself so she can reach.

"I'm going to stay sober in case Julianna needs help with Julian. You can enjoy yourself, though. I can see that Corey is."

I look over and see my sister downing a shot, a separate drink in the other hand. I spoke to my mom about reaching out to her, but all she said was that if Corey wants to speak to her, then she will. She has this old-school mentality where the child should reach out to the parent, which is so ridiculous. Corey deserves better. She shouldn't be the mature one in the relationship trying to fix things, with my mother acting like she hasn't stepped a foot wrong.

I hope she realizes this before it's too late, and she misses out on knowing such a wonderful human.

"At least she's drinking here where people can watch over her," I grumble, picking an olive and cracker from the...what did Bella call it? Grazing platter.

Corey wanders over to us and smiles. "That tequila is good tequila."

And then heads back inside.

Probably to make out with someone in the hallway.

I'm going to mind my own business this time and pretend that she's not even here.

"So when are the two of you going to get married?" Romeo's mother comes up to me and asks the second Bella goes inside. I haven't spoken to Aunty Victoria since last party, and I notice this time she's not drinking as much.

"Next year," I tell her. "I know you didn't mean to tell me what you did last time, but I'm thankful you did. It feels good having everything out in the open."

She smiles sadly. "I'm sorry it came out that way, but I agree. And I want you to know that I only ever felt love for you. I never held anything against you—you were just a child."

"I know," I reply, nodding. She always treated me the same as Romeo, but she never treated him all that great to begin with. "And it is what it is. I just hope we don't have any other family secrets, because I think that one is more than enough."

She laughs but doesn't bother to state that we're all good for now. Because that would probably be a lie.

I go inside to grab a beer and run into Julianna and Damon. Damon is holding Julian and laughing at something Julianna said. The respect the men show Julianna is impressive—it's like she's their queen. And it's so nice to see a woman in power. Maybe soon they will change the rules so women can be official members, too. I can see why Damon would want more men, and more his own age. The older men are slowly phasing out, and depending on how many cousins he has, the numbers might be dwindling.

"When is our wedding?" I ask Bella as she comes out of the bathroom with Corey. I still don't understand why women have to go in packs. "I've been asked, and I don't know."

She laughs. "I don't know either. We'll have to

sit down and decide on a venue and date. Do you want a church wedding? I think I'd like our wedding to be at the lake where you took me swimming that first time."

"The lake sounds good," I say, smiling at the memory, and cupping her face with my palm and bending down to kiss her. "As long as I'm marrying you, I don't care where we are."

"Get a room," Corey comments, and I grin and nod toward our bedroom.

Bella shakes her head, gray eyes dancing with amusement as she gently bats me away from her. "The night is still young. Don't worry, we will end up there eventually."

She's right.

After a few hours, we end up in bed, tearing each other's clothes off.

Is there any other way to end a party?

Chapter Thirty-Seven

Bella

"You're not pregnant anymore, so admit that you're just obsessed with pickles," I say to Julianna, when I find her eating them for breakfast.

She grins and shrugs. "Yeah, okay, fine, I got used to them, and now they're my comfort food. By the way, I had another message from Rosalind, asking if she can meet Julian, and I told her no and blocked her number. The audacity."

"I don't understand why she'd think you would be okay with that after everything she did. She sounds batshit crazy. What is she doing with her life?" I ask.

Julianna shrugs once more. "I don't know, it sounds like she's doing nothing. My parents put her in therapy, which is probably for the best, especially after what happened to Mark. And I think they spend most of their time with her. I know Veronica is in college

now and has moved out of home, so it's just Rosalind there."

"What do they say about her meeting Julian?" I
ask, serving myself some cereal and milk.

"They think I should let her, because what can go
wrong if we are all there?" she imitates, scowling. "I
am not letting my child near her. Knowing what she
is capable of makes me sick. And over a guy she casually slept with? I know his dick is good, but come
on, there's plenty others out there."

I choke on my mouthful, and Julianna has to get
up and slap me on the back. "Don't die on me, Bella.
I need you."

"They say good penis turns women crazy. I think
she is exhibit A," I manage to get out.

"Actually, though," she replies, finishing her last
bite of her pickle, then picking up her coffee, "look
at the time, and Julian is still asleep. This is the first
breakfast I've had to myself since he was born."

"He's such a good baby."

"He is, isn't he? I read somewhere that the first
one is always good, so you want another, but then
the second one is a little demon. It's Mother Nature
playing a trick," she says, an absent smile playing on
her lips. "I'd totally have another, though."

I laugh. "Mother Nature won, then. You know,
River asked me when I would want to have a child."

"And what did you say?"

"Maybe next year? After we're married. But every
time I see him with Julian, I want to change my mind

and get pregnant right now," I admit, lowering my voice. "Hot, muscled men holding babies. Who knew?"

We spend more time talking shit until Julian wakes up, and Romeo comes out holding him. "I can look after him if there's anything you want to do. Or you can go out with Bella and do something? I just have to be at Devil's Play in the afternoon for a meeting with Echo."

Julianna turns to me. "Do you want to go look at wedding dresses?"

"I'll grab my bag," I say instantly. River is outside helping Jag with his motorcycle. "I'm going shopping with Julianna. I'll be back in an hour or three."

"Okay, be careful," he says, opening the door for me and closing it once I'm safe inside.

We check out three different stores and I try on several dresses. When I try on this beautiful mermaid dress, with a low neckline and sequin details, I know it's the one. And when Julianna starts crying when she sees me in it, she confirms it for me.

"You look incredible, Bella. That style is so flattering for you," she raves, doing a circle around me so she can see the whole dress. "River is going to have a heart attack. You honestly look absolutely stunning."

Everyone needs a friend like Julianna. One who will be your biggest supporter and number one cheerleader.

The door opens at the bridal store, the chime garnering my attention. I do a double take as I see none other than Rosalind standing there, looking over at Julianna and me.

"What is she doing here?" I grit out, and Julianna looks over at her sister, instantly standing up.

I put my arm on her shoulder and move to stand in front of her. Julianna may be my president, but this is my fight.

Rosalind walks over with her arms up in the air. "I saw your car in the parking lot, and saw the car seat in there, so figured my nephew might be here…"

"So you thought you'd just show up and hope I'd let you see him?" Julianna asks, stepping to the side of me.

Rosalind crosses her arms against her chest. "He is my blood."

"Yes, and we all know how you treat your blood," Julianna fires back, eyes narrowing to slits.

Rosalind takes a step closer, and my hackles rise. I don't trust this woman, and I don't want her near me or Julianna.

And I definitely don't want her near Julian.

When she's only a few steps away, I, still dressed in my dream dress, step forward and stand toe to toe with her. "Leave, Rosalind. You've done enough. You are not entitled to anything unless Julianna decides it's okay."

"You can't stop me—"

"Why don't you go somewhere where you are wanted?" I fire back.

She winces and looks over to her sister. "Why

won't you let me see Julian? I am his aunty. Whatever we have going on between us has nothing to
do with him."

"You think I'd trust you with my son?" Julianna
replies, exasperation in her tone. "Rosalind, please
just leave me alone. You have done enough. I will
never forgive what you did to Corey. Never."

"I am your *sister*. And no matter what happens, I
am always your sister."

"And that is the only reason you are still alive,"
Julianna snaps, glancing around the store, but luckily the staff members have all disappeared. I can't
imagine how hard this situation is for her, because I
know how much family means to Julianna. But unfortunately you can't choose your family. And Rosalind never cares about anyone but herself. Julianna is
right to keep this boundary, because I wouldn't trust
her with Julian either.

"So that's it? I never get to see my nephew?" she
asks, anger flashing in her eyes. "You're a selfish
bitch—"

My hands flash out before I know. I push her, caus-
ing her to stumble backward. "Leave. Now."

"I'm going to fucking kill you!" She sneers, pulling out a knife from her jeans and holding it out at
me. My eyes widen as I stare at it. "Everyone only
thinks about Julianna! What about me?"

I step back and reach for my handbag, which has
my gun inside.

"Don't move!" she yells at me, her eyes going back

to her sister. "Even Mom and Dad think you are being unreasonable."

Julianna makes a sound of disbelief. "Says you, with a fucking knife in your hands! What the hell, Rosalind?"

I take the distraction and grab the gun out in one smooth move, lifting it up and pointing it at her. If one of us has to die today, it's not going to be me, or my best friend.

Her eyes widen, and she takes a step back, retreating.

And so she should.

She has no care for her sister, for any of us.

She's not a part of our world anymore.

And frankly, I'm so done with dealing with her. First Corey, and now this. Julianna's right—if Rosalind weren't her sister, she'd be dead by now for everything that she has pulled. She is a horrible person, and the world would likely be a better place without her.

"You wouldn't," she whispers, swallowing hard. "Or have you turned into a monster just like River? You know what they say, you are the company you keep."

"The only monster here is you, Rosalind. Now get out of here!"

A customer walks in, a lady who maybe has a decade on us, and Rosalind grabs the woman, dragging her to face us, and holds the knife to her neck.

Fucking hell.

This just went from bad to worse, and I share a look with Julianna, who looks horrified that an innocent woman has now been brought into this. I look over to the manager, who peeps out from the back room, and mouth for her to call the police. She mouths back that she already has.

"Let the lady go," Julianna says in a softer tone. "You don't want to end up in prison, do you?"

The woman looks terrified, eyes wide, silently begging for our help.

"Put the gun down, and I'll let her go," Rosalind says, eyes narrowed to slits. For a moment I consider taking a shot, but I don't want to hurt the woman, and I don't trust my aim right now.

I slowly put the gun down on the floor and push it away with my foot.

Rosalind smirks and opens her mouth to say something when she hears the police sirens. Realizing she's about to get arrested if she's caught, she lets go of the woman and steps back. She then runs out without another word.

"Are you okay?" I ask the woman, who is trembling. The store manager rushes out to help her.

And I hug my best friend, who starts crying, as the two of us calm ourselves. "Holy shit," I say to her, rubbing her back. "Rosalind has lost the plot."

"Put that gun away," she replies, and I quickly pick it up and slide it back into my purse. The police enter, and we all give our statements. I get changed, and we're about to leave when the manager comes out with my dress.

"It's yours," she says, smiling sadly. "Don't let what happened ruin that fact."

She tries to give it to me for free, but I pay for it, not wanting her to lose out on money. I don't deserve a free dress for what happened today. It's our mess that put innocent people in danger, and I don't like that. I feel guilty as hell about it.

I don't let what happened taint the dress, though, just knowing that I won't find another one that makes me look like that.

Even if I've already had to aim a gun at someone while wearing it.

We try to forget Rosalind and all her bullshit, but it's hard. We're both still a bit shaken.

"Thanks for having my back today," Julianna says suddenly, tucking her hair back behind her ear.

"Always," I reply. I love our time together, and I love that Romeo knew that she would need a little break from motherhood, but I know that after today we might not get another one without someone guarding us.

But today we did a damn good job of looking after ourselves, if I do say so myself.

"This is my first time leaving Julian," she admits, checking her phone. "And after what happened, I just want him in my arms. Should we go?"

I nod. "Yeah, let's."

When we walk back into the clubhouse we see River

gently rocking Julian, Hades snuggled up on his left side, obviously supervising, and Romeo coming out of the kitchen with a fresh bottle of pumped breast milk. They both seem to have it all under control between the two of them.

"You're back," Romeo says, smiling widely. His smile drops when he sees our faces. "What's wrong?"

Julianna takes her son in her arms and holds him close. "Rosalind showed up, she pulled a knife, Bella pulled a gun. And then Rosalind took a hostage—"

"But no one got hurt, and we handled ourselves," I add, wincing at the rage I see flash in River's eyes.

"Why didn't you call me?" Romeo demands, frowning. "I'm going to fucking kill—"

Julianna scowls. "Not in front of Julian."

River comes closer to me and pulls me against him. "Are you okay?"

I nod. "I'm fine now."

He looks to Romeo. "I know she is Julianna's sister, but the next time she does something, I'm not going to care."

Romeo looks at Julianna but nods in agreement.

"You can't kill my sister," Julianna says to River, as she takes a deep breath. "I know how crazy that sounds considering everything she does, but I just couldn't live with myself—"

"Just pretend she went on a long vacation," River helpfully remarks.

I elbow him.

"I don't know why she wants to see Julian so bad, but it makes me feel uneasy," Julianna admits. "I hope that she just leaves it alone. I need to tell my parents what happened today. What if we had Julian with us? It's so scary to think he could have been around during all this."

Romeo comforts her, promising that nothing will happen.

"How was Julian?"

"He cried, but we handled it, didn't we, River?" Romeo replies, still watching Julianna with concern etched into his furrowed brow.

River looks over at me with narrowed eyes and says, "Yes, we did. And, Bella, we are waiting a year before we have one of our own like we agreed. Don't look at me like I'm a piece of meat."

I roll my eyes.

He then picks me up, throws me over his shoulder and carries me out. "What are you doing? I have things to do," I call out, squeezing his ass cheeks. He has a really nice ass.

He throws me on the bed, jumps on it and just hugs me, and loves me, kissing my face and holding me tight. "I missed you."

"I missed you, too."

"Why didn't you call me?" he whispers, kissing me. "I would have been over there as soon as I could."

"It all happened so fast," I admit, swallowing hard. "And then it was over. We had a quick drink, because I needed one, and then we came home. Rosalind ran off when the cops came. We had it under control," I say, touching his cheek. I mean, as much as we could have. "I may have lost my temper and pushed her, and then as you heard pulled my gun out on her."

"My sweet, gentle Bella? You've been hanging around me too long."

"That's exactly what she said. But I have to protect the queen," I say, shrugging.

"Well, you are my queen, so next time call me if anything happens," he replies, kissing my nose. "Although after this, I doubt the two of you will be going anywhere without an escort."

I thought as much.

"You know, I think I truly understand you and your need to protect your family and loved ones. There's nothing I wouldn't have done to protect Julianna today. And there's nothing I wouldn't do to protect you."

He stills, and gives me a long look. "And that's why you are perfect for me."

"And I kind of bought my wedding dress," I blurt out.

He rolls me over onto my back and looks me in my eyes. "Really? That was fast. Fuck, I can't wait to see you in it. And then take it off you."

"I know, I wasn't going to buy anything, just try a few on, but when I wore it I just knew it was the one," I say, smiling. "It's stunning."

"Then I'm glad you got it," he says, kissing my

nose. "Anything that makes you smile like that, I want you to have it."

I really do love this man.

I've never felt so loved and so taken care of before. I've never felt more appreciated and more understood.

I've never felt so wanted, and so beautiful.

And that's how I know this is where I'm meant to be.

A few weeks go by with no news from the police, which makes me think that they couldn't come up with enough evidence to take River back in, and I, for one, am thrilled. I don't know what he did to get away with it, and I don't want to know, but I'm just grateful. Maybe I should be scared of him, or concerned about the type of man that he is and what he's capable of, but I'm not. I know that he just does what's needed to be done.

Someone once said that the difference between a hero and a villain is that villains will do anything for the people they love. A hero wouldn't hurt anyone, or kill for someone else.

A villain would.

So maybe he's my villain, and maybe I'm more than okay with that.

He's the most loyal man I've ever known, and he will do what needs to be done for the best of the MC.

For his family.

And I respect that, and him.

And I'd do anything to protect him right back.

So although I come off as sweet and innocent, maybe the truth is that I'm a villain, too.

Epilogue

River

They say when you meet the one you're meant to be
with you'll know.

And I did.

From the moment I laid eyes on her.

I'm sure people say that all the time. But for me,
it's a little different. Before Bella, I never felt a connection with a woman, and I've never found a woman
I wanted to have beside me. I sure as hell never let
one get close to me.

And as I watch her walking toward me, in her
beautiful white gown, I know without a fucking doubt
that this is the woman for me.

This woman is my soulmate.

I never loved before her, and I'll never love after her.

And I know how fucking lucky I am to have found
that in her.

Her long dark hair is down and curly, her lips red
and her gray eyes smoky. She looks like a goddess.

As I stand in my suit, in front of the arbor by a serene lake, I don't feel nervous. I feel excited. We're surrounded by all our loved ones, our family and friends, and I'm glad they are here to share this special moment. A moment I never thought I'd ever be having.

"You look beautiful," I say as she stops in front of me. I can't think of a better word, *beautiful* seems too tame, but maybe there's no words to describe what she is to me.

"Thank you, you look very handsome yourself," she says, smiling up at me. The light she has in her eyes when she looks at me, I never want her to lose that.

We say our handwritten vows to each other, followed by I do.

"You can kiss the bride," the celebrant says, and I kiss Bella like I won her. I dip her backward, putting on a show for the crowd, who all cheer loudly.

And then we walk down the aisle, the wind blowing her hair for the photos, the smiles of everyone we love greeting us. I can't wait to get her home to peel that dress off her.

My wife.

Sometimes the beast can turn into the prince and get his happily-ever-after.

But the best part is when she loves you as the beast more.

* * * * *

Acknowledgments

A big thank-you to Carina Press for working with me on this series!

Thank you to Kimberly Brower, my amazing agent, for having my back in all things. We make a great team, always have and always will.

Brenda Travers— Thank you so much for all that you do to help me. I am so grateful. You go above and beyond and I appreciate you so much.

Tenielle—Baby sister, I don't know where I'd be without you. You are my rock. Thanks for all you do for me and the boys. We all adore you and appreciate you. I might be older, but you inspire me every day. When I grow up, I want to be like you.

Sasha—Baby sister, do you know one of the things that I love about you? You are you. You don't care what anyone else thinks, you stay true to yourself and I am so proud of you. Tahj reminds me of you in that way. Never change. I love you.

Christian—Thank you for always being there for me, and for accepting me just the way I am. Thank you for trying to understand me. We are so different, opposites in every way, but I think that's the balance that we both need. I always tell you how lucky you are to have me in your life, but the truth is I'm pretty damn lucky myself. I appreciate all you do for me and the boys. I love you.

Mum and Dad—Thank you for always being there for me and the boys no matter what. And thank you, Mum, for making reading such an important part of our childhood. I love you both!

Natty—My bestie soulmate, thank you for being you. For knowing me so well, and loving me anyway. I hope Mila sees this book one day and knows her Aunty Chanty loves her so much!

Ari—Thank you for still being there for me, ten years later. You are one of the best humans I've ever known.

To my three sons, I'm so proud of the men you are all becoming, and I love you all so very much. I hope that watching me work hard every day and following my dreams inspires you all to do the same. I love every second of being your mother. You will forever be my greatest blessings.

Chookie—No, I love you more.

Tahj—You make me so proud. You are silently protective of everyone around you. You are smart, and creative. I see you.

Ty—You'll be happy to know I've finished my "working shenanigans" deadline. Love you.

And to my readers, thank you for loving my words. I hope this book is no exception.

About the Author

New York Times, Amazon and *USA TODAY* bestselling author Chantal Fernando is thirty-six years old and lives in Western Australia.

Lover of all things romance, Chantal is the author of the bestselling books *Dragon's Lair*, *Maybe This Time* and many more.

When not reading, writing or daydreaming, she can be found enjoying life with her three sons and family.

For more information on books by Chantal Fernando, please visit her website at www.authorchantalfernando.com.